"Oh," he id you have a b...

"About nine ... er next
to the couch ... back.

Carter nodded, still trying to accept this ... turn of
events. He'd thought Sophia was gearing up to tell him
about a medical issue. But it seemed she'd been trying
to tell him she'd become a mother.

Nine months...

Wait.

His brain kicked in and he started doing the math. He
added up the time since she'd moved, the time since
their encounter.

"But—"

It couldn't be.

They'd used a condom.

He met her gaze, saw the confirmation in her eyes.
She nodded, lips pressed together.

"It's not possible," he whispered.

The baby squirmed in her arms. Sophia turned the
infant around and Carter got his first glimpse of the
little one's face.

His breath stalled in his chest as he saw his own eyes
staring back at him.

"Carter," she said, her voice cracking. "I'd like you to
meet your son."

* * *

Dear Reader,

Sometimes people ask me if I have a favorite book among those I've written. The truth is, I love them all, but some are a little more special to me. Like this one.

Writing this book was a real joy—the story just seemed to unfold in front of me and I had to race to keep up. I love the bond between Carter and Sophia, and how they both come together to parent their son, Ben.

I hope you enjoy getting to know this little family as much as I have. The world has changed considerably since I wrote their story, but love remains constant.

Thanks for reading!

Lara Lacombe

RANGER'S FAMILY IN DANGER

Lara Lacombe

HARLEQUIN
ROMANTIC
SUSPENSE

HARLEQUIN®
ROMANTIC SUSPENSE™

Recycling programs
for this product may
not exist in your area.

ISBN-13: 978-1-335-62884-8

Ranger's Family in Danger

Copyright © 2021 by Lara Kingeter

This edition published by arrangement with Harlequin Books S.A.

For questions and comments about the quality of this book, please contact us at CustomerService@Harlequin.com.

Harlequin Enterprises ULC
22 Adelaide St. West, 40th Floor
Toronto, Ontario M5H 4E3, Canada
www.Harlequin.com

Printed in U.S.A.

Lara Lacombe earned a PhD in microbiology and immunology and worked in several labs across the country before moving into the classroom. Her day job as a college science professor gives her time to pursue her other love—writing fast-paced romantic suspense with smart, nerdy heroines and dangerously attractive heroes. She loves to hear from readers! Find her on the web or contact her at laralacombewriter@gmail.com.

Books by Lara Lacombe

Harlequin Romantic Suspense

Rangers of Big Bend

Ranger's Justice
Ranger's Baby Rescue
The Ranger's Reunion Threat
Ranger's Family in Danger

The Coltons of Mustang Valley

Colton's Undercover Reunion

Doctors in Danger

Enticed by the Operative
Dr. Do-or-Die
Her Lieutenant Protector

Deadly Contact
Fatal Fallout
Lethal Lies
Killer Exposure
Killer Season

Visit the Author Profile page at Harlequin.com for more titles.

This one is for Little Roo and Bub.
Thanks for being my kids!

Chapter 1

"I can't believe this is your last night."

Sophia Burns smiled at Will Porter as she slid his glass across the smooth surface of the wooden bar. The older man was one of her regulars; he'd been coming to Hank's every Friday night for so long, he was practically the bar's mascot.

"I can't pour beer forever." In fact, she felt like she'd already been working here too long. The job had been a nice way to bring in extra cash while she took care of her grandfather, but now that she'd finally managed to convince him to move to an assisted-living facility, she could start living her life again. She didn't regret the two years she'd spent in Alpine, Texas, but in many ways it felt like she'd put her dreams on hold.

But now that her grandfather was settled in and making new friends, it was her turn to move on.

"I know, I know." Will sighed. "You've gotta go look for comets or something."

"Or something," she agreed. There was a temporary lull in orders, so she leaned against the bar for a second. Movement at the far end of the place caught her eye, and she looked past Will on his bar stool to watch Carter Donaghey and the other members of his band as they started to pack up their instruments. They played a set most weekends, and fortunately for her, they were actually pretty good.

Sophia tried not to be obvious as she watched Carter moving around. *What is it about a man with a guitar?* she mused. He was handsome on his own, with his broad shoulders, tanned skin and easy smile. But as soon as his big hands picked up that guitar, he went from appealing to dangerously sexy.

"Think you're gonna find the big one?"

Sophia blinked and refocused on Will. "What?"

"You know." He waved his hand in the general vicinity of his head. "The asteroid that's supposed to take us all out someday."

"Oh." She grabbed a rag and started to wipe down the bar. "I don't know. Anything's possible, I guess."

Will nodded thoughtfully, and Sophia hid a smile. He knew she was moving to El Paso to start the master's program in astronomy at the state university, but she would bet her last dollar his understanding of the subject was limited to alien-invasion movies.

And if the conversations she'd had with people

over the last several weeks were any indication, he wasn't alone in his ignorance.

Carter and his friends moved to the other end of the bar for their postset drinks. She always enjoyed serving them; the guys were polite and friendly and they tipped her well. Moving with her trademark speed, she assembled their usual order and walked it over.

"Thanks, Soph." Danny, the group's drummer, gave her an appreciative grin. He was sweet and single, and when he wasn't playing drums with Carter, he worked as a mechanic. Danny was exactly the kind of guy she should be settling down with, at least according to her grandfather. But while Sophia couldn't deny she liked him and enjoyed talking to him whenever he was around, her affection for him was planted firmly in platonic territory.

"Is this really your last night?" James asked. He lifted his arm as his fiancée, Amy, walked over, and the woman stepped in close for a hug. Sophia couldn't help but notice she'd brought two friends with her, and they were eyeing Carter and Danny with such frank appraisal she felt a sympathetic twinge of embarrassment.

"I head out tomorrow," she replied. Her skin tingled faintly, and she *knew* Carter was looking at her. Sure enough, she glanced over to find him watching her, a smile tugging at the corners of his gorgeous mouth.

"We'll miss you," Danny said. He lifted his glass, and the other guys followed suit. "To Sophia!"

The men echoed his words, and she heard a belated "To Sophia!" from the other end of the bar as Will joined in the toast. She laughed and caught Carter's gaze. He winked at her over the rim of his glass, making her stomach flip-flop.

Not for the first time, she wished she'd had the courage to ask him out. She'd overheard enough conversations to know the sexy musician had a wicked sense of humor and a ready laugh, two important qualities in a man. Given her awareness of him, and the fact that she'd caught him staring at her more than once, they probably would have had fun together.

But she hadn't wanted to form any attachments or put down any kind of roots in Alpine. This was always supposed to be a temporary stop, a stepping-stone on her way to El Paso and graduate school. It had taken eighteen months longer than she'd expected to overcome her grandfather's stubbornness, but now that he was finally settled, she was glad there was nothing else holding her here. She and Carter could have set off some major fireworks, but then she wouldn't have wanted to leave. And as much as she would have enjoyed his company, it was time to start living for herself for a change.

Still, she couldn't deny the sense of wistfulness that came over her as she watched his big hand grip his glass. What would it have been like to feel that body against hers, even just once?

Apparently bored with the conversation, Amy huffed out a sigh and tapped on the drummer's arm. "Danny, have you met my friend Sheila?" She pulled the blonde woman forward, positioning her so that she was closer to Danny. Then she turned to Carter. "And you—" She poked him playfully in the chest with her index finger. "You need to meet Chelsea."

The brunette recognized her cue and moved to stand in front of Carter, thrusting out her chest to better display her prodigious assets. He offered her an easy smile, and they began talking.

Pushing down a rising sense of disappointment, Sophia stepped away and faded into the background again. The logical side of her realized it was silly for her to feel any kind of way about Carter and whom he flirted with. After all, she had no claim on him. They saw each other on weekends, exchanged a few smoldering looks and went their separate ways. Besides, she was moving tomorrow. Pretty soon, she'd be so busy with her studies and her new life she wouldn't even remember Carter anymore.

She knew this, and yet she couldn't stop sneaking glances at him and Chelsea as she counted down the minutes until closing time.

"Do I need to call you a cab?"

Will shook his head as he slid off the stool. "I rode my bike." He weaved a bit as he tried to focus on her. "Left it just outside."

"I don't think you should be riding a motorcycle," she said, but he shook his head.

"Not a motorcycle," he corrected. "My bicycle."

"Oh." She tried to imagine Will riding a bike, but was unsuccessful. "Are you sure you can get home okay?"

He grinned at her, looking suddenly younger. "This ain't my first rodeo, young lady." He pulled his wallet from his back pocket, opened it and withdrew a crisp bill, which he handed to her.

Sophia gaped at the image of Ben Franklin. "Will, no—" It was a sweet gesture, but it was too much. Will's pension didn't amount to much—she knew, because he'd often told her so—and she didn't want to think of him eating cheap ramen noodles because he'd tipped her his grocery money.

He raised his hand, cutting off her protest. "Respect your elders. You've more than earned that. And moving isn't cheap. I know you'll put it to good use."

She blinked back tears, touched by his generosity. "Thank you."

He patted her shoulder. "No, my dear. Thank you. For the last two years, you've listened to my stories and laughed at my jokes. This place isn't going to be the same without you."

"I'll miss you, too," she said. She watched him walk out of the bar and saw him unlock the chain securing a bicycle. Then he climbed aboard and set off, pedaling steadily into the darkness.

She turned back to the bar. Carter and his friends were the only ones left. He glanced up and caught her looking at them. Something flashed in his eyes, but it was gone before she could figure out what. He offered her another one of those lazy, sexy smiles and nodded. Sensing she'd lost his attention, the brunette laid her hand on his arm and leaned close to whisper something into his ear. Carter laughed quietly and dropped his gaze to look at her again.

Sophia sighed softly and started busing the tables. Technically, it was still an hour before closing time, but the place was dead and she wouldn't mind locking up early so she could get some extra sleep.

"Ready to go home?" Carter's voice was low and much closer than she'd expected. Sophia jumped, knocking over the glass on the table she was clearing.

Carter reached around her from behind, his chest brushing her back as he righted the glass. She held her breath at the unexpected contact, which left her feeling even shakier than she had at the initial surprise. She turned to find him standing close, his clear green eyes warm with amusement. "Sorry," he said, though his tone suggested he was anything but.

Sophia felt her cheeks warm and knew she must be blushing. "Nice set tonight," she said, turning back to the table so he wouldn't notice how he affected her.

"Thanks." He reached by her to set the napkin dispenser in the center of the table. "All packed for tomorrow?"

"Yeah." There wasn't much to take. Her clothes fit in the trunk of her car, and she wasn't bringing any furniture since the apartment she was renting in El Paso was already furnished.

"Need any help driving up?"

"Are you offering?" The question escaped her mouth before she could think twice.

He lifted one eyebrow. "Wouldn't have asked otherwise," he drawled.

Butterflies took flight in her stomach at the idea of Carter helping her move tomorrow. Just the thought of spending hours alone in the car with him was enough to make her skin tingle. But though the prospect was highly tempting, she wasn't about to request he give up his entire day to keep her company on the trek northwest. This move was all about fresh starts, not prolonging contact with her crush.

"I appreciate it, but there's no need. I've got it handled."

He opened his mouth to reply, but before he could speak, Amy yelled across the room. "Car-ter." She stretched his name out in a pouty call. "Come back here."

A flicker of resignation danced across his features. Interesting, Sophia thought. Perhaps he wasn't as into the brunette as he'd seemed...

"You'd better go," she said softly. "Don't want to neglect your friends."

He nodded, but made no move to walk away. There was a glint in his eyes that made her think there was something more he wanted to say. She felt herself lean forward, silently encouraging him to speak.

"Carter." There was an edge to Amy's voice now; she wasn't happy he was ignoring her friend.

"Coming." He winked at Sophia, then turned and walked back to the table. "Let's get going, guys," he suggested. "Soph's trying to close up."

"But we still have half an hour!" Amy protested.

"Come on," James said. "It's bad enough Hank

is making her close by herself the night before she moves. Let's give her a break."

Sophia offered him a grateful smile, ignoring Amy's frown and the sour looks on her friends' faces.

"Yeah," Danny agreed, standing and stretching. "I've got an early morning at the garage tomorrow. I should probably get to bed early."

With the three men in agreement, Amy and her friends had no choice but to go along with them. The guys brought their empties to the bar, saving Sophia the extra work. Then James and Danny both gave her hugs as they walked past.

"Good luck," James said.

"Name a comet after me or something," Danny told her with a smile.

Then Carter was standing in front of her, his big, muscular body making her feel small by comparison. "We'll miss you," he said, gathering her in his arms and pulling her close.

Sophia closed her eyes, determined to enjoy this brief moment of contact. His chest was hard against hers, his arms thick bands that held the promise of strength. She inhaled, trying to be discreet as she drew the scent of him into her lungs. He smelled of soap, desert plants and a spicy musk that was his alone. She could spend hours like this and it wouldn't be enough. But that wasn't an option. And since she couldn't very well strip him naked and have her way with him in an attempt to get him out of her system before she moved, she'd have to settle for this.

He gave her a squeeze and released her, his green eyes locked on her as he stepped away.

Sophia swallowed, trying to appear normal. "Thanks, guys. I appreciate it."

She locked up behind them, then turned her attention to the register. It didn't take long to settle everything and put the money and receipts in the safe in Hank's office. As she walked back into the bar, she noticed a jacket draped over the back of a chair.

Carter's, she realized. She walked over, intending to put it behind the bar for Hank to return the next time the band played. But as soon as she picked it up, she brought it to her nose almost reflexively.

She breathed him in, closing her eyes as she inhaled the scent of sagebrush. Her head spun pleasantly, and her heart thumped as she imagined being in his arms again. If only!

A loud rap on the door made her jump. She opened her eyes, still clutching the jacket to her nose. When she saw who stood outside the bar, her stomach dropped.

It was Carter. And he was staring right at her.

Damn.

Carter Donaghey's mouth went dry at the sight of Sophia holding his jacket to her face. It was clear she'd been smelling the fabric, and based on her flushed cheeks and the slightly wild look in her eyes, she liked the scent of him.

Heat flared to life low in his belly, sending tendrils of warmth shooting through his limbs. He'd always thought Sophia was pretty, and he had passed many a night studying her striking red hair, brown eyes and wide smile from his position on stage at the end of the bar. But seeing her now, flustered and aroused, made him realize how sultry she could be.

It only made him want her more.

He'd felt it when he hugged her goodbye—that tug of lust. It had always been bubbling just beneath the surface, but he'd never made a move. He'd known, on some instinctual level, that she wasn't the kind for a casual fling. And thanks to the demands of his job and a complete lack of interest in settling down, he hadn't asked her out. It had been better, easier, to keep his distance.

And that strategy had worked. But now that he'd seen the raw need on her face, he wasn't going to be able to let her go without knowing what she tasted like.

She walked over and unlocked the door, his jacket still in her arms.

A moment of heated awareness shimmered between them.

He stepped inside, shutting them in together. Then he moved closer until their bodies almost touched.

Sophia swallowed hard. "You forgot this." She held up his jacket.

Carter took it from her, then tossed it onto a nearby table. "No," he said, shaking his head. "I forgot this."

He reached out to cup her face with his hands. Her skin was so soft against his palms, her cheeks warm. He dropped his head, then brushed his lips against hers. She sucked in a breath at the contact, and he smiled.

Carter drew back, eyes on her face, as he waited for her response. She tilted up her head, emotions swirling in her beautiful brown gaze. He saw surprise, disbelief, pleasure…and something more.

Desire.

He registered the flash of intent on her face a split second before she moved. The next thing he knew, she was reaching up to thread her fingers in his hair and pulling him down again.

There was nothing hesitant about this kiss. Apparently, she was finished with subtle explorations. This was lust and need and desire given free rein— passion burned so hot it threatened to consume them.

Carter's blood raced south so quickly it left him feeling light-headed. Sophia's hands roamed over his chest, his back, his stomach, her touch setting off tiny spikes of sensations that merged into a wave of intoxicating pleasure.

He gave as good as he got, wanting—no, *needing*— to feel the heat of her skin against his own. Tugging at the hem of her shirt, exposing a stretch of skin to his touch, he ran his fingertips down her side. Pure male satisfaction coursed through him as he felt her shiver against him.

Then she tore her mouth from his and muttered something against his lips.

"What?" He struggled to hear her over the rush of blood in his ears.

"Hank's office," she repeated. She started walking backward, tugging him with her as she moved.

It took a few minutes, and several run-ins with tables and chairs along the way, but they finally made it to the office door. Sophia fumbled behind her for the knob, letting out a grunt of frustration when she couldn't find it. Carter released her long enough to reach behind her and twist it open.

They tumbled into the room together, drawing up short just before crashing into the old desk that sat opposite the door. Sophia pushed him back a few steps until Carter felt his calves hit something. Trusting her, he let himself fall and landed on a threadbare couch. The cushion springs let out a squeak of protest, but the sofa held his weight.

"Stay there," Sophia commanded. She walked to the beat-up wooden bookcase in the far corner of the room and reached for something on a shelf. He caught sight of the label and laughed.

"How'd you know Hank keeps condoms in here?" He glanced down at the couch, evaluating it in a new light.

"It's for the men's-room dispenser," she said, returning with a foil packet in hand. She glanced at his face and smiled. "Don't worry," she reassured him. "Hank doesn't use this sofa for anything other than sitting."

"That's good to know." He reached for her, but she shook her head.

"You take care of that." She tossed the condom onto

his lap. "And I'll take care of this." She moved her hands to her belt buckle and began to loosen her belt.

Carter knew he was supposed to be dealing with the protection, but he couldn't take his eyes off Sophia. Her hands slid down her body, revealing more skin, inch by tantalizing inch. He barely had time to appreciate the sight of her pink lace panties when she dropped them to the floor and stood bare before him.

"Do I need to do everything?" He looked up to see her teasing smile as she gestured to his lap.

Carter simply nodded, his throat too dry to speak. She came forward and knelt between his knees, her nimble fingers working the button of his jeans. He tensed a bit as she tugged down the zipper over his erection, but she moved so carefully he had nothing to fear. Trying to be helpful, he lifted his hips off the sofa and slid down his jeans and boxer-briefs, freeing himself from the confines of his clothes.

Sophia made a low humming sound that sounded like a feminine purr. She leaned forward, and his heart nearly stopped as he felt the tip of her tongue trace his length. He jerked reflexively as she followed the wet trail with those clever fingers, caressing and squeezing in all the right places.

He closed his eyes, seeing stars as she touched him. But as his pleasure continued to build, he grew restless. This was too one-sided; he wanted to touch her, to explore her delectable body with the same attention to detail she was giving him.

He placed his hands on her shoulders, urging her up.

"What?" she asked, her voice sounding dazed. "Is everything all right?"

"Oh, yeah," he growled. "But it's my turn now."

He pulled her onto his lap so she was straddling his legs. Then he lowered his hand, touching her intimately as he kissed her again.

As he stroked her most sensitive places, she squirmed against him, emitting soft sounds of pleasure as he brushed his thumb over her. He captured the sounds with his mouth, dipping his tongue inside to taste her as she gasped for breath.

Her hips moved rhythmically, and he could tell she was searching for release. Her words confirmed it a second later. "Please," she whispered breathlessly. "Don't make me wait."

Carter took his hands off her body long enough to slip on the condom. Then he grabbed her hips and guided her into position.

She sank onto him with a groan, biting her bottom lip as he filled her. He could have stayed like that forever, surrounded by her warm heat, but then she began to move, rocking with a pace that made his eyes roll back in his head.

"I'm not gonna last long," he warned, panting between each word.

"Me, neither." She gripped his shoulders tightly, her short nails digging into his skin. The subtle pain only served to heighten his pleasure, a delicious combination that chipped away at his control.

He could tell she was getting close, too. Her movements changed, her pace becoming more frantic as she chased her release. He reached between their bodies to stroke her sensitive nub with the pad of his thumb.

That was all it took. Sophia threw back her head and moaned his name, her body clenching around him as her hips slowed and then stilled.

Watching her surrender completely was the sexiest thing he'd ever seen. Knowing he was the cause of it pushed him over the edge. He gripped her tightly and held her in place as he thrust up into her.

The moment seemed to last forever, pleasure arcing between them like an electric current. Slowly, gradually, he came back to earth. Sophia slumped against his chest, her body now limp and boneless in his arms. It felt as though they had melted together, and to be honest, the thought of remaining attached to her all night long didn't bother him in the slightest.

He wasn't sure how long they stayed that way, her head on his chest and his arms wrapped tightly around her body. Finally she stirred, pushing up to look at him with sleepy, satisfied eyes.

"Did we just—?" She sounded as though she couldn't quite believe it.

"Yeah." He laughed, feeling just as surprised. Now that he knew how good they were together, he was kicking himself for not having suggested this sooner. "Do you really have to move tomorrow?"

She smiled, but he saw a twinge of regret cross her face. "I do." She looked down, shook her head. "How's that for timing?"

Carter reached up and tucked a strand of hair behind her ear, pushing aside a sense of disappointment over their missed opportunity. "What's that line? At least we'll always have Paris?" He wasn't going to pretend they could make a long-distance thing work. His work as a park ranger in Big Bend was intense, and he knew she was about to start a master's program. She wasn't going to have time for romantic entanglements, and he'd rather walk away with this cherished memory than watch their connection wither to nothing over the next few months, with all the hurt feelings that would accompany their decline.

"Something like that." Sophia climbed off him, and they spent the next few minutes putting themselves back together. They didn't speak, but the silence wasn't awkward or embarrassing. He felt comfortable around her, and it wasn't just the aftereffects of the great sex they'd just shared. She'd always put him at ease, even when she was simply watching him from across the bar while he played with the guys.

"I wish we had more time." They walked out of the office together, and she closed the door behind them. He wasn't just talking about tonight, either. Even though they'd just slept together, he already wanted her again. It was going to take more than one encounter to get her out of his system.

But since that wasn't an option, he was looking at a future of cold showers.

"Me, too." She smiled up at him. "I had no idea things would be so...intense between us."

Yeah, that was a good way to put it. So was off

the charts. Their chemistry was undeniable, a force to be reckoned with.

They walked to the door together, and she flipped off the lights before they stepped outside. He watched as she locked up, the streetlights in the parking lot bathing her in a pale glow.

"Are you sure I can't help you move tomorrow?" It would only be prolonging the inevitable, but he'd take whatever time he could get.

Sophia shook her head. "That will only make it harder," she said. "Let's just say goodbye now, while things are still simple."

She was right, and he knew it. So he stepped forward and wrapped her in a hug. She squeezed him tightly, making his heart stutter in his chest.

"I'm going to miss you," he said softly. "And not just because of the sex."

She laughed, her chest vibrating against his. "I feel the same way about you."

Carter released her, knowing she needed to go. "If you ever come back to visit your grandfather, look me up." Maybe they couldn't have a serious relationship, but he wouldn't be opposed to a friends-with-benefits situation. Anything to keep her in his life.

A mischievous look crossed her face. "Now that I know what you're capable of, I think I will."

Before he could laugh, she rose to her tiptoes and planted a quick kiss on his lips. Then she turned and headed for her car, leaving him standing by the door.

Carter watched her walk away, his amusement fading into a suspicion that he'd just let something wonderful slip through his fingers.

Sophia waved at him as she drove out of the parking lot. He waved back and set out for his truck, shaking his head at the unexpected turn this night had taken. A breeze kicked up, making him shiver as the cold air danced along his skin.

"Dammit." The realization hit as he reached his truck, and he put his head on the glass of the driver's-side window, kicking himself.

His jacket was still in the bar.

Chapter 2

One month later...

Carter opened his eyes and immediately wished he hadn't. Sunlight speared his retinas with the precision and intensity of a laser beam, making his eyes water. He blinked and tried to raise his hand to shield his face.

But his arm wouldn't obey his brain's commands. *What the—?*

He tried to move again, and that was when the pain hit. A wave of agony rolled over him, stealing his breath. His vision fuzzed into gray despite the sun's brightness as every muscle and bone in his body screamed for attention. For a few seconds his world went black as his brain seemed to short-circuit in the face of so much bombardment.

Then he was back, consciousness returning with a fresh surge of torment. He took a breath, trying not to scream as his chest expanded.

Am I dying?

The words cut through the haze, a bright flash in the corner of his awareness. He could feel his mind shrinking, collapsing into a kind of primitive state as it tried to process the overwhelming damage to his body. It was a terrifying sensation, feeling his thoughts disappear in the wake of every agonizing heartbeat, every shaky breath.

He tried to swallow, registering the coppery taste of blood on his tongue. Grit coated his mouth, the back of his throat. He felt it in his nose, too. God, maybe he was drowning in it.

There was a thunderous grating sound to his right. Then a shadow fell over him. His heart leaped in his chest, his body instinctively reacting to the unknown danger.

Not that he could do anything about it.

Carter heard a noise above him, though he couldn't place it. He squinted, trying to determine what was standing over him.

Finally, it hit him.

A face.

As soon as he realized it was a person looking down at him, a switch flipped on inside his head and he understood what he was hearing.

"Oh, my God. You're alive!"

Carter tried to speak, but it was too much work.

"Don't talk," the man said. "Please, don't do anything." He ran his gaze down the length of Carter's body, and Carter could tell by the look in the young man's eyes that things were bad.

It wasn't exactly new information, but he felt a tingling of panic at the base of his spine. If someone else was here, seeing him like this, then he wasn't having some kind of strange, hyperreal nightmare. This was actually happening.

He *was* dying.

"I'm going to take your walkie-talkie," the young man said. "I've got to call for help."

Carter felt a tug on his belt as the guy pulled his radio free. He heard the urgency in the man's voice as he made contact with someone and begged for help. When he was done, he placed the radio on the ground and loomed over Carter once more.

"You hang on, okay? They'll be here soon."

Carter tried to smile, appreciating the young man's attempt at encouragement. But he knew on a visceral level that while help was on the way, they wouldn't be quick. Big Bend was too remote for that.

Things were starting to come back to him. Nothing terribly helpful, just snippets of memories flitting on the edges of his awareness. If he tried to focus on images, they faded into nothingness. So he avoided chasing them too hard. Gradually, a picture began to emerge.

He'd been on patrol. Where, though?

Didn't matter. He'd been walking—that much he remembered. And thinking of Sophia.

The vision of her face danced through his mind

once more, and for a moment, the pain receded. She was beautiful, intoxicatingly so. What he wouldn't give to see her again! Especially now, knowing he didn't have much time left. Why hadn't he approached her before? They could have had months or even years together, instead of that one breathless encounter.

Anger and sadness surged, causing Sophia's memory to fade from his mind. He'd been so afraid of being tied down, of missing out on having fun with his friends and his music, that he'd passed up an opportunity to experience something extraordinary with her.

"You fell." The young man's voice cut through the chaos of his thoughts. "I was on the trail, about a half mile under you. I heard you yell, and when I looked up, I saw you fall off the ledge." He ran a hand down his face, still clearly shaken by what he'd witnessed.

The words triggered a memory. "Snake." Carter's voice was hoarse, barely more than a whisper. He grimaced and swallowed reflexively, but it didn't help.

Fortunately, the young man heard him. "Rattler?"

Carter didn't bother to try to speak. He simply blinked in acknowledgment. He remembered now— he'd been walking, lost in thought. The telltale rasp of the snake had been his first clue that he was in trouble. Rather than stay calm, he'd reacted on instinct, jumping back in a bid to get away from the animal. Too late, he'd realized his mistake. His careless reaction had taken him right over the edge of the narrow trail, sending him flying through the air. His stomach heaved as he recalled the nauseating weightlessness of the free fall. He'd barely had time to curse his own stupidity before he'd hit the ground and his world had gone black.

The man shook his head. "Oh, man. Were you bit?"

"Don't think so," Carter rasped. Though at this point, did it really matter? He'd fallen at least thirty feet, onto the rocky trail below. Everything hurt, and there was no telling what kind of internal damage he'd sustained.

With effort, he pushed aside the cynical thoughts. He was in a tough spot, to be sure. But that didn't mean he should give up.

"Can you drink?" The young man held up his water bottle. Then he frowned. "Do you think it's okay to have water in your condition?"

"Can't hurt," Carter said.

The water was deliciously cool in his mouth. His rescuer was careful to give him small sips, making sure Carter swallowed before giving him more. After he'd had enough, Carter closed his eyes and shook his head ever so slightly.

The guy sat back. "Okay," he said, clearly thinking out loud. "Let me see if I can get some shade for you. Do you have anything in your pack?" He reached for Carter's backpack, still trapped under his body. But he yelped before the young man could move him.

"I have to stay still," he said, the words coming easier now that the water had soothed the parched tissues of his throat. "I didn't mean to scare you, but you can't move me."

Awareness dawned in the guy's eyes. "Ohhh," he said, nodding. "I get it. Spinal injury, right?"

Carter pressed his lips together for a second. "Probably." But not something he wanted to think about right now. First things first—he needed to survive until the medevac arrived. Then he could worry about all the other stuff.

Like if he'd ever walk again.

"I have a jacket in my bag." The man pulled a windbreaker free from his pack. "Maybe I could hold it over your face? It'd be better than nothing." He settled next to Carter's head, stretching the fabric out so it cast a bit of a shadow.

Carter smiled. It was a nice gesture, even though it wasn't helping much. "What's your name?" he asked. They were going to be stuck out here for the foreseeable future. Might as well make the best of it.

"Rob," the young man said. "I go to school at Tech. We're on a fall break, so I came out here to do a little exploring."

Carter shifted slightly, triggering a fresh wave of pain. He grimaced and tried to breathe through it. "I'm glad you were here," he choked out.

"Me, too," Rob said. "Is there anything I can do for you? Something to help while we wait?"

"Talk to me," Carter replied. "Just talk." He could use the distraction. He needed something to take him out of the broken shell of his body, to occupy his thoughts so he didn't spiral into a black hole of self-disgust over his foolish mistake.

Rob started talking, jabbering nervously about his major and the classes he was taking.

He's a good kid. Too bad he has to see this.

Carter shifted again, his body seemingly unable to stay still. It was as if his muscles had wrested control from his brain and were determined to move in the hope of finding a new position that might relieve the relentless pain.

It didn't work. Carter felt something give in his chest, accompanied by a fiery stabbing sensation that made him see stars. He groaned, nearly passing out again.

Rob loomed over him once more, his face gone pale despite the heat and the sun. "What is it? What's happening?"

"Don't know," Carter groaned. He took an experimental breath, trying not to exacerbate the situation. Immediately, he knew that something was wrong. He felt like he was trying to breathe through a wet cloth—he couldn't seem to draw in enough air to expand his lungs.

Great, he thought to himself. *I've gone and punctured a lung.* At least, he hoped that was all he'd done. He'd had enough medical training to know there were many other injuries that caused a stabbing chest pain.

"What do you need? What can I do?" Rob's voice had gone up an octave, hysteria edging his words. Carter realized he needed to give this kid a job, or he was going to panic.

"Keep talking," he said, trying not to gulp for air. "Tell the medics I need a chest tube. On my left side," he rasped.

Rob's eyes went wide. "That doesn't sound good. Can you breathe? Do I need to do mouth-to-mouth?"

In any other situation, the question would have made Carter laugh. As it was, he felt the corners of his mouth lift. "No," he gasped. "It's okay." It was clear his condition worried Rob, and he genuinely appreciated the young man's desire to help. But at this point, there was nothing to do but wait.

Rob rocked back on his heels, still distressed. He was quiet for a moment. "Do you still want me to talk?"

"Yes," Carter croaked. A niggle of doubt was working its way through his brain. Sure, he wanted to live. But maybe he'd suffered too much damage. Maybe there was nothing to be done. Could these really be his last moments on earth?

Rob started talking again. Carter ignored the words and instead focused on the sound of the young man's voice. If he was going to die, at least he wasn't alone. Though truth be told, he wished he could have seen Sophia one last time.

Breathing was getting harder. His vision was starting to grow fuzzy on the edges. *They're coming*, he told himself. *Just a little longer.*

But it was so bright outside. Maybe he could rest his eyes until the medics arrived. What could it hurt?

He closed his eyes. From far away, he thought he heard a yelp of alarm. *What was that?*

Didn't matter. He pictured Sophia's face, smiling up at him. In his mind, she reached for him.

He took her hand, releasing his hold on consciousness to drift away with her.

* * *

This can't be happening.

Sophia stared at the pregnancy test in her hand, refusing to believe her eyes.

Two pink lines.

Pregnant.

"No." She practically threw the stick on the bathroom counter and began to pace the small room. "It's not possible."

She'd only slept with one man in the last six months. Carter Donaghey. An explosive onetime encounter the night before she'd left that still gave her goose bumps whenever she thought about it.

It had been an uncharacteristic move on her part; one-night stands usually weren't her thing. But she'd made an exception then, driven by her long-standing desire for Carter and feeling emboldened by the knowledge she'd never have to see him again. She'd figured if they didn't click in bed, they wouldn't have to deal with any awkward run-ins at the bar later.

Except they had clicked. Very much so.

A shiver raced through her as the memories came to the forefront of her mind. The feel of his large hands on her skin, his touch gentle but his fingers and palms just a little rough from the calluses he'd earned playing guitar and working as a park ranger. The sound of his voice, deep and melodic. And the way he'd gasped when she'd—

Sophia cut off the thoughts before she got lost on memory lane. Her encounter with Carter was in the past. And that was where she had expected it to stay.

"We used protection," she said, talking to herself. "I watched him put the condom on." And she knew he hadn't tricked her, because she'd seen him dispose of it after they were done. They had been responsible, because neither one of them had wanted their fun to result in a pregnancy.

It didn't, she decided, shaking her head. There was another explanation for this result. The test was faulty. That had to be it.

She headed for the kitchen, pulled a bottle of water from the fridge and drank it down in a few gulps. While she waited for it to work its way through her system, she mentally reviewed all of the other reasons why her period was late.

The stress of the move.

The stress of starting her graduate program.

The stress of trying to meet people and make new friends.

That was it. All the recent changes in her life and the worries they had brought had thrown off her cycle. It happened all the time.

But twenty minutes and two tests later, her resolve crumbled.

Sophia sank onto her couch, feeling numb as the realization took hold.

She *was* pregnant.

Now what?

The next three days passed in a blur of tears and sleeplessness. Sophia cycled through every possible emotion, one moment feeling amazed and in awe of the fact that she had a little life growing inside of her, the next minute balled up on the floor of her apartment, crying her heart out as abject terror took hold. Eventually, her mood evened out, likely due to the fact that she was so totally exhausted she could no longer muster the energy to do anything but sit on the couch and stare into space.

The timing of this pregnancy couldn't be worse. Sophia had a five-year plan all mapped out for her life. First, she was going to finish grad school. After earning her master's degree, she was going to focus on getting her dream job at NASA. Then once she had her career on track, she'd turn her attention to finding a man and settling down to begin a family. Babies were step four of her plan. She was still at step one. Her brain refused to accept that she was skipping over several crucial milestones.

The logical side of her knew that having a baby would upend her whole life, forever altering her tidy plans for the future. And given the fact that she'd already put her dreams on hold while taking care of her ailing grandfather, Sophia couldn't deny that the prospect of doing so again was decidedly unappealing. Perhaps she was being selfish, but this was supposed to be *her* turn. Her chance to do what she wanted, to work toward the goals she'd been nurturing for so long.

Not to mention, she'd been raised by a single mother. Her father had walked out when she was only two, leaving her behind without a second look. Her mom had been left to do everything by herself—working full-time, cleaning, cooking, washing, doing all the errands. As Sophia had gotten older she'd helped as much as she could outside of school and sports, but she knew all the years of exhaustion had taken their toll on her mother.

Did she really want to sign herself up for that kind of life? There was no guarantee Carter would want anything to do with this baby. Was it fair to bring a child into the world, knowing he or she might not have a father?

This should be an easy decision. She was pregnant, and she didn't want to be. She didn't have to be for much longer.

It wouldn't take much to deal with this situation. She hadn't yet found a doctor in El Paso, but there was a women's health clinic nearby. She could make an appointment, do what was needed to have her life go back to normal.

It was the logical thing to do—the safe thing to do if she wanted to pursue her dreams.

But what if it wasn't the right choice for her? her heart whispered.

They'd used protection. They'd taken every precaution. And yet she was still pregnant. Sophia wasn't a big believer in fate, but perhaps it was time to make an exception. Maybe this baby was supposed to be here. Maybe this was the universe's way of telling her that this was her time to become a parent, not years from now, as she'd planned.

The thought took root in her mind and started to

grow. If this was her chance to be a mother, could she really afford to pass up the opportunity?

Having a baby would change everything. All her carefully crafted plans for the future would have to be reevaluated. But…not all change was bad, was it? She'd still be able to pursue her degree—women had babies and went to school all the time. It would be hard, but not impossible.

And she could still get that job at NASA. Maybe not on the time line she'd envisioned, but she didn't have to stop working toward her goals simply because she'd had a baby.

As for the husband and family parts, well, that might be a little trickier to manage. Not every man wanted to date a single mother. But, she realized with a growing sense of resolve, she wasn't interested in dating every man. The right one would want her and her child. He'd love them both, and he'd be a good father to her little one.

She sat with the idea of a baby for a long time, lying quietly on the couch as she poked and prodded at the edges of the thought, trying to decide how she felt about it.

Life-altering. That was the only way to describe the choice she faced. Sophia felt like she was literally standing at a crossroads; no matter what decision she made, her life would never be the same.

Could she afford to have this baby?

Could she afford not to?

Sophia had never been one to back down in the face of a challenge. In high school, she'd tried out for the softball team on a broken ankle. She'd thrown up in the bathroom before the auditions for the school musical, but she'd rinsed her mouth, wiped her face and walked out on that stage like she owned it. When her grandfather had needed help, she'd stepped up to the plate to take care of him. She was tough. Determined. Competent. If anyone could handle the demands of juggling graduate school and having a baby, it was her.

"Looks like this is going to be my next adventure," she said softly. She placed the palm of her hand on her belly, embracing the new life within her. "What do you think? Shall we go for it?"

She didn't get an answer. Hadn't expected one, really. So she was surprised when a powerful sense of peace fell over her, calming her jangling nerves and filling her with confidence.

"This is right," she said to herself. "This is the right choice for me."

It would be hard, there was no doubt about it. But in Sophia's mind, anything worth doing was challenging.

She walked into the kitchen, grabbed a pad of paper and a pen. Time to make a list, so she could take control of this situation and stop feeling like a victim of circumstances.

First things first; she needed to find a doctor. And get some vitamins—weren't pregnant women supposed to take special vitamins?

She'd need to tell the graduate program. She had a year's worth of classes to complete before starting her thesis. Maybe they would work with her and let her double up on some of the courses so she could get them done before the baby was born.

The extra bedroom she'd originally intended to use as her home office was going to have to be turned into a nursery. That meant getting a crib and a dresser. And diapers. How many diapers did a baby need? She made a note to do further research on that topic.

Baby clothes. The kid couldn't be naked all the time. And a car seat, so she could go places. Probably a stroller, too.

Her stomach dropped as she added more and more items to her list. She wasn't exactly made of money, and the graduate-student stipend didn't leave much for extras.

"I'll make it work," she muttered. Not everything had to be new. There were thrift stores in El Paso— she could shop there for the things the baby would outgrow quickly.

And…maybe Carter would help her?

He'd be just as shocked as she was to find out about the pregnancy. God, had he even thought of her in the weeks since she'd left? Or was he dating that brunette from the bar, Celeste… No, Chelsea had been her name.

"Carter and Chelsea," she said, wrinkling her nose at the bad taste left in her mouth. She couldn't really begrudge him if he was dating that woman. They'd made no promises to each other. But the thought of being replaced so quickly did nothing to improve her mood.

Regardless, she needed to tell him. It was his baby,

too, and he deserved the opportunity to be a father, if that was what he wanted. After all, not every man was like her dad, who'd been all too eager to walk away from his responsibilities.

She reached for her phone, then just stared at it as she realized she didn't have his number. They hadn't exactly exchanged contact information before parting ways.

No problem, she thought. Everyone was on social media these days. She'd just find him that way.

Thirty minutes later, she shoved her laptop across the table with a sigh. Carter was apparently one of the few people who didn't have social-media accounts. It made sense, she mused. Big Bend was a huge tract of wilderness—he didn't exactly have regular internet access while at work.

So how could she get in touch with him? His bandmates would probably have his number. She knew the shop where Danny worked as a mechanic—she could call there and talk to him.

It didn't take long to find the number. She took a deep breath, her stomach fluttering with nerves once more. It was one thing to decide she was going to keep the baby. But it was something else entirely to tell Carter he was going to be a father.

Sophia punched in the numbers before she could change her mind. A spurt of panic rose in her chest as the call went out. What was she going to tell Danny? She couldn't exactly say she wanted Carter's number so she could tell him their one-night stand had resulted in a permanent connection. She had to come up with an excuse, and fast…

"Rickey's Garage."

Oh, God, it was Danny on the line. She wasn't even going to get a minute to compose her thoughts while someone grabbed him from the garage. She bit her lip and plowed ahead.

"Hey, Danny, this is Sophia. I, uh, tended bar at Hank's?"

There was a beat of silence. She cringed at her awkwardness, wishing she was the kind of person who was cool and composed. Then Danny spoke, rescuing her from her self-doubt. "Oh, yeah, hey, Soph! What are you up to? How's El Paso treating you?"

The warmth in his voice brought tears to her eyes. "It's good. Different from Alpine, but good."

"What can I do for you? Got a question about your car?"

Because why else would she be calling him? She smiled at his assumption, wishing that was the reason for her call.

"No, my car is okay. I was actually hoping you could help me get in touch with Carter…" Her voice grew softer as she spoke, leaving her whispering at the end.

"What?" Danny asked. "Sorry, it's kind of loud in here. I didn't hear you."

Sophia closed her eyes. She repeated her question, then held her breath as she waited for Danny to respond.

"Carter? Oh, Soph, I don't have the number for his

hospital room. You could probably call the medical center and ask. But I don't think he's in any position to answer the phone right now." He sounded sad, and she imagined he was shaking his head as he spoke.

Sophia felt the bottom drop out from her stomach. "What? What do you mean his *hospital* room?" She tightened her grip on the phone, straining to hear.

"You didn't know?" She heard the note of confusion in Danny's voice. "Then why—?"

Her throat tightened, making it hard to get the words out. "Danny, what happened to Carter?"

"He fell off a trail. I think it was a thirty-foot drop. A hiker found him, called in for help. They barely made it in time. He's pretty beat-up—broken leg, broken pelvis, ribs. Cracked some vertebrae. He's got a concussion and punctured a lung. They took him in for surgery right away. Said he has a long recovery ahead of him."

The words washed over her, the horror of Carter's condition sinking in by degrees.

"Soph? You still there?"

She shook herself free. "Yes," she whispered. She cleared her throat and spoke louder. "Yes, I'm still here. When did this happen?"

"Yesterday morning. Surgery was in the afternoon. I think they took out his spleen?" He sounded uncertain. "Anyway, they said he did well but he's going to need a few more operations before all of this is over."

"Oh, my God. I can't believe it." Carter had talked to her about his job before, how much he loved being a park ranger. Some of the other park rangers were regulars at the bar, and from what she'd overheard, Carter was well liked.

"Yeah," Danny said with a sigh. "From what I've heard, it was one of those freak accidents."

"Is there anything I can do?" El Paso was several hours away from Alpine, but maybe she could drive back this weekend. It sounded like his doctors were taking good care of him, but perhaps there was some way she could help him?

"I don't think so." Danny's voice was kind. "His sister flew in last night. She's staying by his side, and James and I were there yesterday. The waiting room looked like a park-ranger convention—I think everyone who works in Big Bend was there."

"That's good." Sophia tried to smile through her tears.

"Carter would want you to stay put and focus on grad school," Danny continued. "But I'll tell him you called when I see him."

"Thanks," she said. "Would you do me a favor?"

"Sure," he replied easily. "What do you need?"

"Will you please keep me posted and let me know how he's doing? Can I call you every few days? Just until we know he's going to be okay?"

"Of course. I'd be happy to."

"Thanks, Danny."

"Anytime. Listen, try not to worry about him. You know how stubborn Carter is. He's going to get through this. You just focus on your studies and find that asteroid before it takes us all out."

Sophia laughed weakly. "I'll do my best."

She ended the call and leaned back in her chair, still trying to process this news. When she'd last seen Carter, he'd been physically perfect, strong and tall, full of energy and life. It was hard to imagine him broken and fragile, his body damaged.

Tears slid down her cheeks as her heart broke for him. They'd danced around each other for as long as she'd worked at Hank's, chatting between his sets or between her customers. They hadn't spent a lot of uninterrupted time together, but they'd always found each other in the lulls of those nights. She'd felt a connection to him, a pull that was almost magnetic. And unless she missed her guess, he'd felt it, too.

She skimmed over the memories of their hot encounter, a hint of sadness coloring the edges now. Carter had been in his physical prime, a man who was comfortable in his own skin. Would he ever be the same? Would his body fully heal? And if not, how would that affect him mentally?

So many questions, but no answers in sight. It would probably take weeks, if not months, for Carter's doctors to gauge his recovery, to know if he was going to make it back to normal.

Surgeries, physical therapy… He'd probably have to learn how to walk again, thanks to all the broken bones. He'd definitely have to learn how to live in his body as he mended, which was no small feat.

Sophia shook her head, her mind made up. Carter had his hands full, and then some. He had his own battles to fight, and given his precarious condition, it was going to take all his energy and focus to get better. The last thing he needed right now was the added pressure of knowing he was going to be a father. If they'd been in a relationship, news of the baby might have come as a welcome surprise, might have given him the motivation to get better. But since they'd only engaged in a onetime fling, word of this pregnancy would likely only upset him. Sophia didn't want to add to his problems right now. So for the time being, she was going to keep this secret to herself.

Later, once Carter had recovered, she'd tell him about the baby. He deserved to know he was a father, and she didn't want to keep him in the dark forever. But for right now, he needed to heal.

Which meant she was on her own.

Chapter 3

Eighteen months later...

"**Y**ou're doing great, Carter. Just a few more feet." Carter winced as he shuffled forward, his grip on the handle of the cane so tight he thought he felt it crack.

"You gotta keep breathing, man."

At the reminder, he exhaled, then drew in another cautious breath. His ribs still ached from time to time, especially when he was exerting himself.

Like now.

Carter had lost count of the number of hours he'd spent in physical therapy over the last year and a half. They'd started while he was still in the hospital. From the moment he'd opened his eyes, confused and still feeling fuzzy from the anesthetic, someone had been there, encouraging him to move, twisting and angling his body in various positions in a bid to help him heal.

At first, it had seemed like torture. The doctors were still doing surgeries, trying to patch him back together. "Why can't you leave me alone for a few days?" he'd grumbled.

But that hadn't been an option. "No can do," one of the therapists had said. "The sooner we get you started, the faster you'll recover and the more function you'll have."

They'd been right, of course. But that was small comfort in the face of the agony he'd endured.

Carter had been lucky. The physical therapists he'd worked with had been wonderful. Truly caring people, who knew when to push him and when to ease up a little. Still, deep down, Carter was convinced they were all a little barbarous. How else to explain their relentless cheer in the face of his discomfort?

"Almost there…"

He made it to the chair, turned and sank down onto the seat with a deep exhalation. Moving slowly, he carefully relaxed his hold on the cane, giving his body time to adjust to the new position. He'd learned the hard way that quick transitions resulted in painful flares.

"Great job!" Mike, his outpatient physical therapist for the last nine months, gave him an encouraging smile. "You're getting faster."

Carter nodded, feeling pleased with himself. Progress was slow, but given the extent of his injuries, he knew he'd already come a long way.

Some days, he still couldn't believe he'd survived.

The medics had arrived in the nick of time and whisked him away to the hospital, where the doctors and nurses had pulled out all the stops to save him.

"You're lucky," one of the surgeons had said a few days after Carter had been admitted. "I think you're going to make it."

At the time, he hadn't felt so lucky. His thoughts had been fleeting and scattered, thanks to the concussion. But in his more lucid moments, fear had taken hold of him as he'd looked down at his bandaged and mangled body.

Will I ever walk again?

On the heels of that thought had come another: *Can I return to my job?*

He didn't know what he would do if he couldn't go back to being a park ranger. It was more than just a job to him—it was his life. He loved being outside in the wilderness, exploring the remote areas of the park, helping visitors discover the magic of nature. There was no way he could sit at a desk, cooped up inside all day. He needed to breathe the fresh air and feel the warmth of the sun on his skin.

His medical team hadn't balked when he'd told them he needed to make a full recovery. They'd listened to his worries, and with serious faces they'd told him they could make no guarantees. But if he was willing to put in the work, they would do everything in their power to see that he was able to resume his normal life.

It had been an uphill battle. On his bad days, Carter wondered why he was even bothering to try. He could barely walk twenty feet without his hips and legs and back screaming in protest. Was he ever going to get rid of this cane? Or was he going to hobble around for the rest of his life, a disabled old man at the age of thirty-two?

But then he had good times. Moments of triumph, when he reached a goal or made measurable progress. He still remembered the first time he'd walked to the bathroom unassisted. Such a seemingly simple task that he'd taken for granted for most of his life. Now he had a deep appreciation of the coordination and strength it took to cross that distance.

Before the accident, Carter had always assumed his body would work the way it was supposed to. He'd never had any reason to think twice about moving or bending or reaching. It had been effortless, almost instinctive. He'd wanted to do something, so he'd done it.

He didn't have that luxury anymore. The accident had forced him into a new relationship with his body. He had to think about everything—the best way to stand, the proper way to stretch or twist or grasp. He could no longer trust that his muscles and bones would know what to do without conscious input.

It was exhausting. It was demoralizing.

And for a while, it had been horribly depressing.

Fortunately, his sister, Margot, had seen the change in him. Someone had contacted her after the accident, and she'd flown in to be with him. Her face had been the first thing he'd seen when he'd opened his eyes in the hospital. And she'd stayed, always by his side, advocating for him, pushing him to work hard so he could recover.

At first, he'd had a hard time communicating with her. Margot was Deaf, and he hadn't been able to sign very effectively. But she'd come prepared. She'd used the talk-to-text feature of her cell phone, so she'd been able to read what he and others were saying. It wasn't a perfect system, but as time had passed, Carter had been able to start signing again.

He didn't know where he'd be without his sister. Margot had known he needed help, and she'd encouraged and then downright nagged him to talk to a therapist. His medical team had recommended a counselor, and Carter had agreed to talk to them. The sessions had done wonders for his mental state, giving him the tools he needed to understand and accept his new reality and make him feel like he could still live a full life.

"All right, let's go again."

Mike's words snapped Carter out of his reverie. "Now?" he complained half-heartedly. "I just got here."

"Yep. And we need to go back to the other side."

"We?" Carter repeated. "Who is this 'we' you speak of? You got a turd in your pocket or something?"

Mike blinked and then laughed as Carter braced himself to stand. "Can't say I've heard that one before."

"My dad used to say it to me." Carter got to his

feet and positioned his cane. "When I was a kid, my sister loved to go to the movies."

"Isn't she Deaf?" Mike asked, moving next to Carter for the journey back across the room.

Carter nodded. "She is. But she still loved watching Disney movies. And the volume was so loud she could feel the vibrations in her seat."

"Makes sense."

"Anyway, I'd go ask my dad. 'Can we go to the movies?' And he'd look me up and down and say 'We? You got a turd in your pocket or something?'"

Mike shook his head. "I bet you loved that answer."

"Oh, yeah. It got old real quick." He focused on his steps, making sure he was balanced before he took the next one. "But more often than not, he'd take us. Just had to get his dad joke in first, you know?"

"He sounds like a character."

"He was," Carter confirmed.

"Is your sister still in town?" The question was innocent, but there was a note of forced casualness in Mike's tone.

Carter turned to look at him appraisingly. "She is." He normally lived in park-ranger housing inside Big Bend. But thanks to his regular therapy and doctor's appointments in Alpine, he and Margot were renting an apartment nearby.

They reached the other chair and Carter turned to sit once more. Mike reached for one of the therapy balls and passed it to him. Like the dutiful patient he was, he began his next set of exercises.

"Is, uh, is she working?"

"Yes. She's doing some interpreting at the hospital and some local doctor's offices. It's not full-time, but it keeps her busy."

"That's good," Mike said.

Carter raised an eyebrow. "Were you hoping to bump into her?"

Now Mike's cheeks flushed. "Would that be a bad thing?"

"Not at all." Carter smiled. "I'm not her keeper. She's a grown woman. She can do what she wants."

"Yeah, but I'm your therapist. I don't want to be unprofessional."

Carter waved away his concern. "She's not your patient. You can't be the first physical therapist who is attracted to the family member of a patient."

"That's true," Mike said quietly. "But if you think it's inappropriate, I won't ask her out."

"You'll just wait until I'm done?" Carter said, half joking.

Mike nodded, his expression serious. "Yep. My priority is helping you. I don't want to do anything to jeopardize your progress."

"I could always switch therapists."

"You could," Mike replied. "But I hope you don't." A grin slowly spread over his face and his eyes glinted with amusement. "I'm the only one who wants to put up with you."

Carter laughed, the unexpected movement making his ribs ache. But it was worth it. "Go for it," he said. "She's picking me up when we're done. I'll make sure to introduce you properly."

The remaining half hour of physical therapy passed in a blur as Mike led Carter through the rest of his exercises with his trademark blend of encouragement and sarcasm.

"I'm gonna feel this later," Carter remarked, dabbing his forehead with the towel he'd brought.

Mike grinned. "That was the plan."

"Sadist," Carter grumbled.

"I've been called worse," he said with a shrug. "Listen, I want you to keep doing the same leg exercises at home, but increase your reps to twenty-five. Morning and evening. Got it?"

"Look, man, whatever I did to offend you, I'm sorry."

Mike laughed. "Trust me. You're making good progress. Can't rest on your laurels now."

Carter chuckled and got to his feet. He started for the door, then stopped and looked behind him. "You coming or what?"

Mike practically leaped forward to catch up. As they walked, he smoothed his hand over his hair. "Do I look okay?" The note of worry in his voice was almost endearing.

"Not really," Carter said. "You look like yourself."

"Very funny." Mike harrumphed as they pushed through the doors into the waiting room. His sister was sitting in a chair on the far side of the room, reading one of the out-of-date magazines from a nearby rack.

Margot looked up as they approached. She smiled at him, nodded at Mike and picked up her phone, ready to communicate.

Carter began signing, speaking as he did so for

Mike's benefit. "Margot, I'd like you to meet my therapist. This is…" He trailed off as he realized Mike's hands were moving.

"Hello," the other man said as he signed. "My name is Mike." He painstakingly spelled out each letter. Carter didn't have the heart to tell him he'd spelled his name as *M-i-k-a*.

Mike held his hand at an angle, fingers outstretched and palms flat. He ran one palm across the other, then closed his hands into fists and extended his pointer finger up. He brought his fists together, then pointed at Margot. *It's nice to meet you.*

Carter felt his eyebrows rise. It was clear his therapist had more than a passing interest in Margot. He'd obviously been researching sign language and had taken the trouble to learn some basic signs.

Margot's eyes lit up. She slowly signed back her response. *Nice to meet you, too.*

Mike smiled. *Do you want to get a drink with me sometime?*

Yes. She nodded enthusiastically. She handed Mike her phone and made a typing gesture.

Carter stepped back to give them a few minutes to work out the details of their upcoming date. It warmed his heart to see his sister so animated. He knew she missed her friends in Austin. They videochatted regularly and texted all the time, but it wasn't the same as actually going out to do something fun.

Mike had surprised him, in a good way. The fact that he'd taken the time to learn a bit of sign language was encouraging.

Carter watched the two of them, heads bent together as they passed the phone back and forth. He smiled to himself. Maybe this was the start of a relationship for the pair? Years from now, he could tell their kids he'd seen it from the beginning.

Would he ever have that? Before the accident, he'd entertained thoughts of finding a wife and starting a family. Now he wasn't so sure. Physically, he was still a long way away from recovery. Women weren't exactly lining up to date a guy who couldn't walk more than ten minutes without needing to sit down.

And as for kids, well, he wouldn't be much help in that arena. Children needed to be active—to jump, run, play. He'd seen dads at the park with their kids, watched them lift those little bodies to reach monkey bars or slides. Carter wasn't supposed to lift anything that weighed more than a backpack, which meant he'd be relegated to the sidelines. Of course, if he did have children, he'd have years to build up his stamina and conditioning. But he needed a partner first, which brought him back to the fact that his social life had been put on hold in favor of learning to walk again.

But now that he was on the road to recovery, maybe it was time he started enjoying life once more. There was no reason why he couldn't go out on dates—well, except for the fact that he hadn't met anyone yet. It shouldn't be too hard to meet women, though. He just had to make an effort.

His thoughts drifted to Sophia, as they often had in the months since she'd moved away.

Once he'd known he was going to survive, he'd

thought about reaching out, getting in touch with her again. After all, when he'd thought he was dying, he'd kicked himself for not having taken a real shot with her before. But every time he'd considered looking her up, he'd stopped himself. She'd moved to El Paso to chase her dreams and didn't need a man from her past intruding in her new life. Especially one with so many issues of his own to deal with. Besides, he wasn't quite sure what he wanted from her. Was he hoping she'd drop everything and return to Alpine to be with him? Not going to happen. Could he be happy as her long-distance friend? Someone she spoke to every once in a while, if she ever felt homesick for the dusty little town she'd left behind? No, that wouldn't work for him, either. It was selfish, he knew, but he wanted more from her than that.

In his heart of hearts, Carter wished they had taken a chance back when they'd both had time to explore the connection between them. If he'd overcome his reluctance to commit, cast aside his determination to keep his relationships light, they might have built something together. Hell, maybe he wouldn't have even gotten hurt in the first place if they'd been dating. It had been thoughts of their encounter that had distracted him, kept him from seeing that rattlesnake until it had been too late.

Could've. Would've. Might've. But who really knew? It was just as likely that the chemistry he'd felt with Sophia was a short-term thing, a flame that would have burned hot and bright and then fizzled. Still, if that had been the case, at least he'd have had the benefit of closure. Of knowing they'd taken that chance, given it their best shot. Instead, Carter was haunted by the memories of how good she had felt in his arms and an aching sense of loss for the road not taken.

He shook his head, casting aside the glum thoughts. It was easy to get caught up in regrets, in the possibilities of what might have been if he'd made different choices. But he couldn't live in the past. The door to the therapy rooms opened again as a patient walked through. The faint sound of guitar music drifted into the waiting room, probably from a music-therapy session. Carter's mood lightened as an idea formed in his mind. Danny and James still played together, though no longer at the bar. Maybe they could get the band back together? Play a few sets at Hank's, for old times' sake?

He knew his guitar skills were a little rusty—he'd started strumming again at home, though not practicing in earnest. But it shouldn't be that hard to get back up to speed once more. His arms and fingers hadn't been all that damaged in the fall, and if he needed to, he could sit on a stool to perform. His heart lightened at the thought of playing music with his friends again—it would feel so good to get out and be around people, to soak in the energy of the crowd on a Friday night while he and his buddies created a kind of magic on the stage. And maybe, just maybe, he'd meet a woman he wanted to spend some time with.

He pulled his phone from his pocket and fired off a message to his friends: Wanna start playing again?

Within minutes, both Danny and James texted back.

God, yes.

Just been waiting for you to say the word.

Carter laughed to himself, happy to know his friends were on board. When can we get together?

Danny responded: Tonight? I'll stock up the fridge with drinks.

I'm in, texted James.

I'll bring the pizza. Carter paused, then continued typing. You know I'm a little rusty, right?

We all are, James fired back.

Hasn't been the same without you, replied Danny.

Relief filled Carter's chest as he read his friends' responses. Part of him had worried they'd moved on, perhaps decided they no longer wanted to play or, worse, no longer wanted to make music with him. He wouldn't have blamed them. Still, it was good to know he could recapture this part of his life once more. Things would never truly go back to the way they'd been before he'd taken that fall. But he still had his music.

That was enough for now.

Two weeks later...

"I can't believe he left you a house."

Sophia shook her head and watched as her cousin, Leah, walked around the living room, stopping to examine the contents of the bookshelves that lined one wall. "I know," she said, moving to join the younger woman. "I'm still in shock myself."

"Remind me how you knew this guy?"

Sophia reached out to straighten a book. "Will was a regular at Hank's, when I tended bar there. He came in every night, sat on the same stool and sipped on a couple of drinks until closing time. I'd listen to his stories between customers. He was a sweet old man, clearly looking for company. But never in a million years did I think he'd do something like this."

Leah cocked her head to the side. "I think it's kind of cool. I mean, you clearly meant a lot to him for him to give you all his earthly possessions."

"I suppose." Tears pricked Sophia's eyes as she thought of Will. How lonely he must have been, to leave her, a relative stranger, everything he owned!

Leah ran her fingers along the back of a sofa, the upholstery clean but worn. "Do you think he was in love with you?"

Sophia rolled her eyes at her cousin's flight of fancy. Leah was seventeen and steadily working her way through her mother's collection of romance novels. "No," she said firmly.

But Leah wouldn't give up. "Are you sure? Because this is the kind of thing that only happens in the movies. Or in books. In fact, I'm reading this novel now, where the heroine inherits a castle from a relative she didn't know she had. She moves there and finds out the bank is trying to repossess the place. The bank agent is this tall, brooding guy who never smiles. And—"

"Let me guess," Sophia interrupted dryly. "They fall madly in love?"

"Of course," Leah replied, as if this was the most obvious thing in the world. "But right now they're still angsting for each other."

"Angsting?" Sophia repeated. "I didn't know that was a word."

Leah arched one eyebrow, looking like a prim teacher. "We studied Shakespeare in English class this year. If he can make up words, why can't I?"

Sophia couldn't help but laugh. "That's a fair point."

Leah accepted her reply with a nod and continued to roam around the room. "What are you going to do with all of this stuff?" She raised her arm, waving to indicate the collection of furniture, books, knick-knacks and other miscellanea Will had accumulated over his lifetime.

"I have no idea," Sophia said with a sigh. "I don't even know what all is in the house." She'd only arrived a couple of days ago, after hitting pause on her life in El Paso.

Will's lawyer had called her two weeks ago with the news of the older man's death. Sophia had barely had time to process the information before the attorney had dropped the biggest bombshell: Will had left everything to her. His home, his car, the balance of money in his bank account. Everything.

"I d-don't understand," she'd stammered over the phone. "Why me? Surely he must have some relatives?"

"This was what he wanted," the man had explained. "He said you were always kind to him. He wanted you to use his assets to make your life easier."

"So he wanted me to sell his house?"

"That's entirely up to you," the attorney said gently. "I'd recommend you come to Alpine and take stock of everything. Then you can decide what you want to do."

She'd spent the last two weeks talking to her professors, explaining the situation. Her adviser had understood. "Go," she'd said. "You're due for a break. You worked hard to pass your qualifying exams, and you can wait a bit to start your research full-time."

Sophia had been so grateful she'd nearly started crying in the woman's office. "Thank you," she'd said.

Dr. Kuban had smiled. "Sophia, you don't need to thank me. You've been burning the candle at both ends, doubling up on classes to fit everything in while still taking care of your son. I'm a mom, too. I know how hard it is to balance things. This is the perfect time to hit pause—we'll be here when you get things in Alpine sorted out."

So she'd tied up loose ends in El Paso—talked to the day care, her landlord, put her mail on hold. She'd also spent time on the phone with Will's attorney, discussing the legal implications of her new assets. He'd drawn up a will for her, one that left everything to her son. And he'd offered guidance on how best to approach the monumental task before her.

"I can help you," Leah volunteered now, pulling

Sophia from her thoughts. She shrugged. "I mean, if you want."

Sophia smiled. "Is this really the way you want to spend your last few weeks of summer vacation?"

The young woman nodded. "Yeah. I don't mind." She ran her gaze over the bookshelves again. "Looks like he had some interesting stuff. It'll be cool to go through it all."

"I would appreciate the help," Sophia said.

"Can I hold the baby, too?" Leah asked.

Sophia blinked at the non sequitur. "Of course." She hadn't expected Leah to be all that interested in Benjamin, but in the two days since she'd been back in Alpine, Leah had spent a lot of time playing with Ben, feeding him and just generally cooing at him. For his part, Ben had enjoyed the attention, grinning and squirming in delight when Leah was around.

Leah grinned. "He's really sweet."

"He is." Warmth spread through Sophia's chest as she pictured her baby, currently asleep in the Pack 'n' Play in the bedroom. She loved everything about him, from his soft, red-brown baby hair to his adorable little toes. He had the chubbiest cheeks in the history of babies, and when he smiled, her heart ached with love for him. He was the best thing that had ever happened to her, and every day she was grateful to be his mother.

In her eyes, Ben was perfect.

He was also deaf.

"I'm trying to learn some sign language," Leah continued. "I checked out a book from the library, and I've been watching some videos online. But I don't know much yet."

Sophia smiled at her cousin. "That's okay," she said. "I'm still learning, too."

Leah was quiet for a moment. "Are you going to get him a cochlear implant when he gets older?"

"I think so," Sophia replied. "If his doctors say he's a good candidate for it. I want him to be able to have some sense of hearing."

"You don't think he should be left alone?"

Sophia frowned slightly at the question, wondering what her cousin was getting at. "What do you mean?"

Leah shrugged. "I've been doing some research. Some Deaf people think cochlear implants and hearing aids are unnecessary. That you don't need them to be happy."

Sophia stared at the young woman, surprised by the depth of her interest. "You really have been looking into this. Why?"

Twin spots of color appeared on Leah's cheekbones. "I just think it's interesting," she said. "We talked about Helen Keller in school a few years ago. She was really inspiring. And now that I know Benji…" She trailed off, then glanced at Sophia shyly. "I think I may want to learn sign language so I can become a teacher for Deaf kids."

"Seriously?" Surprise washed over Sophia. She hadn't expected Ben's condition to spark such a reaction in the young girl.

Leah's face fell. "Never mind. It's a dumb idea."

"No, it isn't." Sophia reached out and put her hand

on Leah's shoulder. Her cousin looked up at her, a spark of hope in her eyes. "I think it's a wonderful idea. I think you'd be a great teacher. And I'm glad Ben has inspired you to learn more about deafness." It was a journey she was taking herself—one she was finding held many twists and turns and bumps in the road.

Sophia had never faced anything like this before. Having a baby was hard enough. Knowing her son was different was an additional challenge, something that she was still trying to accept.

Ben's birth had been uneventful, as far as any birth ever was. There had been no signs that he was anything other than perfect. But the next day, he'd failed his initial hearing screen. Still, they'd told her that sometimes happened and not to worry. But when they'd tested him again just before sending them home and the results had been the same, Sophia had known something was wrong.

After several visits to the pediatrician and some additional screening, the diagnosis had been made: sensorineural hearing loss. Something was wrong with the structures in Ben's inner ear, preventing sounds from being communicated to his brain. Since Sophia hadn't had any issues during her pregnancy, the doctors thought it was most likely due to genetics. After Ben's birth, she'd done a little research into her family tree and discovered a great-aunt she'd never met had been Deaf. The realization had been surprising, but part of Sophia had been a little relieved to have some kind of explanation for her baby's condition.

"How long are you going to stay?" Leah asked, bringing her back to the here and now.

"I'm not sure," Sophia admitted. It was going to take some time to go through everything in the house and to get the place ready to sell. But she had another task ahead of her, one that made her stomach clench every time she thought about it.

It was time to introduce Carter to his son.

True to his word, Danny had given Sophia updates about Carter's recovery. From what she'd heard, he'd had a difficult time of it. Several surgeries, lots of physical therapy. But he was living in an apartment in Alpine now, with his sister helping him. It was clear that he was going to be okay, even though he would probably never go back to the way he'd been before the accident.

She should have told him about Ben months ago, once she knew that Carter was improving. But after getting Ben's diagnosis, she'd spent several months just processing the fact that her baby was deaf. She'd been thrust into a new and unfamiliar world, one full of doctor's appointments, parent support groups and classes to help her communicate with her baby. Never in a million years had Sophia thought that becoming a mother would mean she needed to learn a new language. And this was all in addition to her graduate studies. She'd been overwhelmed, and just the thought of telling Carter about the baby had been stressful enough to make her cry.

Things were better now. She was still coming to terms with Ben's condition, but she no longer felt such acute grief for the loss of possibilities his deafness had initially meant to her. She was learning, through her own research and her interactions with the parents of other Deaf children, that Ben's lack of hearing didn't doom him to a sad, bleak life. He would be able to do pretty much anything a hearing child could—play, learn, make friends. His deafness wouldn't prevent him from forming meaningful connections with people or keep him isolated and alone. There would be challenges, to be sure, but Sophia was going to do everything in her power to make sure her son had the same opportunities as everyone else.

But what would Carter think?

It was a question she returned to often, one that kept her up at night. Finding out he was a father was going to be a huge shock. Finding out his son was deaf would be another blow. How would he respond? Would he welcome the news and open his heart to Ben? Or would Ben's deafness give Carter an excuse to turn his back on his son?

Her own father had walked away when she was a child, and she hadn't had any health issues. Could she really expect Carter to help, given the fact that he was still dealing with his own recovery?

It was the fear of Carter's rejection that worried Sophia the most. Every time she looked at Ben, a fierce sense of protection, nearly overwhelming in its intensity, filled her. She would do anything for her baby, no matter the cost. If Carter walked away from him, she wasn't sure how she'd handle it. Just the thought of Carter hurting Ben that way made her blood boil.

Sophia didn't have many memories of her own father, certainly nothing that stood out in her mind. Despite his absence, her mother had done an amazing job making sure she'd felt loved and secure. Growing up with such an incredible role model gave Sophia the confidence to know she, too, could do this on her own if necessary.

"You okay?" Leah's question snapped Sophia out of her reverie. "You look kinda sad."

Sophia gave her a wobbly smile. "I'm good. Just… feeling overwhelmed."

"Can I ask you something?" Leah looked away as she ran her finger along the edge of a shelf, leaving a small clear path in the dust.

"Sure," Sophia replied. The young woman was helping her organize the house—the least she could do was answer a question for her.

Leah took a deep breath, as if fortifying herself. "Where is Ben's dad? Why isn't he helping you with this?"

Sophia sighed, wondering if her cousin had some kind of psychic powers. What should she say? She'd been very close-lipped about the details of Ben's father, not telling anyone his identity for fear of the news getting back to Carter before she was ready to tell him herself. As a consequence, she knew her family had formed their own conclusions about things. Her aunts had called her up several times during her pregnancy, dancing around the subject but refusing to ask point-blank.

"I'm just glad your mother isn't here to see this, God rest her soul," her aunt Linda had remarked at one point. "Her only daughter, in trouble like this!"

Their scolding had set Sophia's teeth on edge, but she'd tolerated it for the sake of peace. Her aunts were her only remaining connection to her mother, who had died five years ago. And while there were times the three women made her want to tear out her hair, she knew that, for all their faults, they did love her. They'd sent her care packages since Ben's birth, boxes of diapers and bottles and baby clothes. No one in her family was rich, but they'd all done what they could to help her and make sure Ben had what he needed.

She didn't owe anyone but Carter an explanation. But now that she was in town, intending to give Carter the news, did she really need to keep the secret anymore?

"Ben's father doesn't know about him," she admitted, deciding to open up a bit. "That's one of the things I need to do while I'm here. I was hoping to introduce Ben to his dad."

Leah's eyes widened. "Oh, wow. That's huge."

Sophia nodded. "My thoughts exactly."

"How do you think he's gonna react?"

Sophia shook her head. "I wish I knew."

Leah paused, then said, "You know, I read this book a few weeks ago. The hero was a spy, and he fell in love with the heroine while on an undercover mission. He had to leave suddenly, but she never knew why he disappeared. She found out she was pregnant a few weeks after he left. Fast-forward three years later, and he came back to find her again. Except now she has a kid and he thinks she moved on after he left."

Sophia smiled, drawn in by the story despite herself. "So what happens?"

"He's upset at first. And he doesn't understand why she's not falling into his arms. But he eventually explains why he had to leave, and she forgives him for abandoning her. At first, he was mad that he had a kid he didn't know about, but he gets over it."

"And they wind up together?"

Leah nodded vigorously. "Oh, yeah. He's excited to be a dad, and she's happy to be with him again. It all works out."

"That's good," Sophia said softly. It was a nice story. If only her life would turn out as well!

"It was dicey there for a while," Leah continued. "But they kept talking and eventually they trusted each other again."

"Maybe that's the moral of the story? To keep talking."

"I think so." Leah sounded thoughtful. "That's one thing I've learned from reading these books. Bad things happen when you don't talk to the person you love."

Sophia blinked, taken aback by her cousin's words. It was a profound lesson to have learned at such a young age. If she was being honest with herself, it was a lesson Sophia was still trying to learn.

Chapter 4

Jake Porter stepped off the bus in Alpine, squinting in the midday sun. It felt good to move after spending the last two days on a bus, though he wished he was stretching someplace a little cooler, say on a beach populated by bikini-clad women. Instead, he was here, breathing in the dusty air and wishing for a shower.

He hadn't wanted to come here. Childhood visits over the years had convinced him he'd seen and done everything that Alpine had to offer. And he couldn't care less about the landscape or driving down to Big Bend for some camping. Why sleep outside in the heat like a fool when there was air-conditioning available?

No, he was here for one thing only: money. Hopefully the old man would give it to him without a fuss and he could be on his way again.

Jake walked into the bus station, making a beeline for the bathroom. There were no showers, but a quick wipe-down with some wet paper towels left him feeling marginally better.

He headed into the main room of the station, which had a large city map hanging on the far wall. He studied it for a few minutes, a little surprised to find the town had grown a bit since he'd been here last. It still wasn't anything special, but it looked like there were a few more dining options and several new stores around.

Whatever. He wasn't here for shopping or to sample the local cuisine, such as it was.

It rankled that he was even here at all, but after that last run of bad luck, he'd been forced to take a step back and regroup. It was fine, though. He was down, but not out. He'd top up his accounts and then head home again so he could win back his money.

A thin smile stretched across his face as he imagined the shocked faces of the dealers as they realized the tables had turned. The house usually won, but Jake's luck was about to change. He could *feel* it, a tingle of certainty that he was going to start winning again.

Things were already getting better. After his last big loss, when he'd staked his car in a private game that he was now certain had been rigged, he'd grabbed his duffel from the trunk and taken a walk to clear his mind. He hadn't paid any attention to where he was going, but when he'd looked up again, he'd been standing in front of the bus terminal. The universe had led him there, guided him toward his path back to solvency.

Without another thought, Jake had bought his ticket and hopped on board, realizing only after the fact that he'd signed up for two days of sitting in his own funk. In the larger scheme of things, it was a small price to pay. He didn't mind getting a little dirty for his money.

First things first, though. He needed a vehicle. Alpine might not be a big city, but he couldn't walk everywhere. And, more important, he needed to project a certain image when he went to visit his grandfather. If the old man thought he was irresponsible or desperate, he wouldn't help him.

"I'm not going to give you money just to have you waste it on gambling!" Will Porter had insisted.

The words echoed in Jake's ears, his grandfather's parting sentiment from their last visit several years ago. Jake had come through town on his way to Vegas, hoping for a little help.

"I'm a safe bet, Grandpa," Jake had argued. "I know what I'm doing!"

Will had shaken his head, mouth set in a thin line. "You need to forget about that and get a job. Do some work for a living, something you can be proud of."

"I am working for a living," Jake had retorted. "I'm a professional gambler. This is what I do!"

His grandfather had looked confused at that. "You mean like those men who play poker on television?" he'd asked, frowning.

Relief had filled Jake; maybe his grandpa wouldn't be so hard to convince after all. "Yes, exactly like that."

But Will had shaken his head in dismissal. "That

doesn't seem like a real job. And even if it is, what do you need money for?"

"I'm heading out to Vegas," Jake had said. "I've done all I can do in Atlantic City." Technically, that had been true. He'd maxed out both his credit and his patience for the Atlantic City scene. Things had started to get dicey, so he'd decided to leave while he could still walk. He'd stopped at some of the reservation casinos along the way, earned back some money to pay off most of his debts. Enough so that no one would come after him, anyway. Then he'd set his sights on Vegas, the center of it all.

He had an image to maintain, though. It wouldn't do to arrive with nothing. He'd needed to make a big entrance, to attract the attention of the high rollers so he could get in on their games. Big risk, yes. But also big rewards.

If his grandpa would have fronted him the money, he could have dived right in to the scene, started playing immediately. None of that working up from the bottom, wasting time with the low-stakes nonsense the tourists preferred.

For a moment, it had seemed like Will was going to help him. But then the older man had sighed.

"I don't understand you," he'd said, sounding a little sad. "You've already spent your inheritance from your father. He's been gone only five years, and you've already burned through his life-insurance money."

Jake had bristled at the words. "That wasn't my fault—"

But Will had cut him off. "It is," he'd said firmly. "You're not a boy any longer, Jake. You're a man. Take responsibility for your actions. Own them!"

"I am!" Jake had yelled. "I've paid off my debts and I'm looking to start fresh. You act like that's a bad thing. What more do you want from me?"

The older man's eyes had glistened with tears as he stared up at him. "I want you to find a steady job. Meet someone special. Build a family with them. I want you to be happy."

Jake had swallowed his frustration. Meeting people wasn't a problem—there were always women in the casinos, eager to befriend anyone on a hot streak. He'd passed many a pleasant night with them, celebrating his wins with hours of debauchery that would make a sailor blush. But never, not once, had he felt the desire to settle down, to commit to any one person.

"I am happy, Grandpa," he'd said, trying to be gentle. "This is my life. It's what I want to do. It's what I'm good at."

Will's face had hardened then, and Jake knew he'd disappointed the man. "Then go," his grandfather had said. "Do what you want. But I'm not paying for it."

They hadn't spoken since that visit. And Jake wasn't sure how he would be received now. But he knew one thing—he couldn't go begging, hat in hand. If his grandfather thought for one second he was asking for money to go back to Vegas and pick up where he'd left off, he'd slam the door in his face without so much as a hello.

No, Jake had to play his part. Had to make it seem like he'd turned over a new leaf, that he was starting a new life. He'd had a lot of time to think on the bus ride to Alpine. It was probably best to pretend that he had a job—a real one—and that he was saving up for a down payment on a house. When his grandpa wanted to know why he was staying in Vegas rather than moving away from temptation, he'd tell him the company needed him there.

It was a good story. Jake had considered adding a girlfriend to sweeten it a bit, but decided he didn't want to press his luck. His grandfather would want to see pictures of the two of them together, and there weren't any photos on his phone he wanted the older man to look at.

Jake scanned the city map, looking for a car rental place. He found one about two miles down US 90, next to a motel. Perfect. He'd get a car and a room, clean up, then head out to see his grandfather.

He snagged a bottle of water from the vending machine and stepped outside. It was hot as hell, but the walk would do him good.

"Hi, Grandpa," he said, rehearsing as he plodded down the side of the road. "I'm back."

"You ready?"

Carter glanced at Danny and nodded. "Yeah. I think so." They were in the parking lot of Hank's bar, watching people walk in. Their instruments were in the back of Danny's truck, and in a matter of moments, they'd be setting up on the small stage inside. He was going to play in front of people for the first time since the accident. It was enough to make his stomach flutter with a combination of nerves and excitement.

James clapped him on the shoulder. "We're gonna have fun tonight."

Carter nodded. "I know."

"Nervous?"

Carter shrugged. "A little," he admitted. They'd been practicing together for the past week, but he was still feeling a little rusty. He didn't want to wait any longer, though—it would be good to reclaim this part of his life, even if only for a few hours.

"Don't be. Lots of friendly faces will be in the crowd," Danny said. He slid a glance toward James, who bit back a smile.

What was that about? Carter frowned, studying his friends. "I feel like I'm missing something here."

"Not at all," Danny said smoothly. "Come on. Let's get going." He opened the door and climbed out of the truck. James followed suit, hopping down easily.

Once upon a time, Carter would have slid off the seat without a second thought. But now he moved carefully, slowly arranging his legs into the correct position and using his cane for stability as he transferred his weight from the seat to his feet.

Danny and James were already at the back of the truck, pulling out instruments. Carter shuffled over to join them and reached for his guitar case.

James lifted an eyebrow. "You sure?"

Carter merely cocked his head to the side. He'd told the guys earlier that if he needed help, he'd ask for it.

James nodded, looking sheepish. "Yeah, okay. Sorry."

He held out the guitar and Carter wrapped his free hand around the handle. "Thanks."

"Let's go, boys," Danny said. He secured the tailgate back into position and the three of them set off across the parking lot. Carter was slow, but his friends matched his pace so he wasn't left to walk by himself. It was a nice gesture that he appreciated.

The neon signs in the front window buzzed softly as Carter stepped up to the front door. He pulled it open, letting the cool air wash over him as he entered.

He took a deep breath, inhaling the familiar scents of grease and hops. The bar seemed both bigger and smaller at the same time. He eyed the stage at the back end of the place, wondering if it had always been that far away, or if he'd simply never noticed because he'd never had to think about walking before.

The air hummed with conversation, the occasional peal of laughter rising above the din. There were a lot of people here tonight. Carter glanced around, his heart tripping a little as he realized all the tables were occupied.

"About time you lot showed up," Hank grumbled. He was behind the bar, serving a steady stream of customers. "You said you'd be here at eight."

Carter glanced at the clock hanging high on the wall. It was only five past the hour, but apparently that was late enough to ruin Hank's mood.

"Sorry," James said blandly. "Traffic."

Danny snickered and Carter bit back a smile. One of the benefits of living in a town the size of Alpine was a general lack of congestion. The old-timers liked to gripe about the steady increase in the number of people living here, but compared to cities like El Paso and Austin, Alpine was downright quaint.

Hank shot them a dark look and walked to the end of the bar, drying his hands on a rag as he walked. He eyed Carter up and down in frank appraisal. "How are you doing, son?"

Carter recognized the concern underlying the older man's gruff tone. "Better every day," he replied honestly.

Hank nodded. "That's good to hear." For a second, he looked as though he wanted to say something else. But then he jerked his chin toward the stage. "Get to it, ladies. Time's a'wastin'."

The three of them headed toward the stage. People smiled as they made way, nodding in greeting. A few clapped Carter on the back as he walked past. "Good to see you again," one man said.

"Glad you're back," a woman uttered from somewhere close by.

Carter smiled in acknowledgment, grateful for their words. He'd been worried that people would no longer want to hear him play, but that didn't seem to be the case.

It took a few minutes to get everything set up. Carter focused on the task at hand, blocking out the noises of the crowd as he worked. His nerves subsided as he lost himself in the familiar motions. By the time he was done, he felt almost normal again.

"You guys ready?"

Danny and James nodded. "Oh, yeah," James said with a grin.

"Let's do this," Danny added.

Carter looked at his friends, warmth spreading through him as he soaked up this moment. He was back. It wasn't quite the same as it had been before—his cane leaning against the wall was a reminder of that—but he was well on his way. The accident had taken a lot from him, but through hard work and perseverance, a ton of help and a little luck, he was making his way back to the things he loved.

His friends smiled at him, apparently also caught up in this palpable moment of pulse-pounding anticipation. Carter gave them a nod, then turned around to face the crowd and stepped up to the mic.

"Evening, folks."

His voice rang out in the room. The crowd hushed, heads turning to look at the stage.

"We're Tall—" He couldn't finish the band introduction as a roar rose from the crowd. People clapped loudly, whooping and hollering, grinning up at him. A wolf whistle pierced the air, adding to the noise.

He took a step back, overwhelmed by the reaction. In all the time he'd spent missing the joys of performing, he'd never considered the possibility that people might miss hearing him play.

The residents of Alpine had been amazingly supportive during his recovery. Fortunately, it wasn't every day a park ranger experienced a near-fatal accident. His story had made the news, and the community had rallied around him. There had been fundraisers to help pay for his medical expenses, offers of help and collections of handmade cards from the kids in elementary school. People had been quick to reach out, and the generosity of the town had truly humbled him.

Carter felt tears sting his eyes in the face of such a rousing welcome. He wiped his hand down his face, unable to do more than stare at the crowd.

Hank stood in the back, watching him with a small smile. Carter gave him a little wave, and the older man nodded in acknowledgment. Then he made a shooing gesture with his hands, as if to say "get on with it, boy!"

Recognizing his cue, Carter stepped to the mic once more. After a moment, the cheers died down and a sense of expectation filled the room as people waited for him to say something.

He cleared his throat, hoping he could speak. "That was…" He trailed off, shook his head. How could he find the words to thank everyone? To express how much their support meant to him? Maybe if he had more time he could come up with something eloquent. But now, in the heat of the moment, he was going to have to improvise.

"That was just about the best welcome any man could hope for."

The audience began clapping again. He looked out over a sea of smiling faces, wondering how in the world he'd gotten so lucky. The accident had taken a lot from him, true, but he'd also enjoyed some beautiful moments, experiences he never would have had if not for the fall.

"I know you didn't come here to stare at me," he said. A chuckle rose in the room and the applause died down again. "What do you say we play some music for you?"

Hoots and hollers of support gave him the answer. Carter half turned to check in with Danny and James. They both nodded, faces alight with grins.

Carter counted them off quietly. "One, two, three…"

They began playing in unison, strumming the familiar riff of a classic rock song. A cheer rose up from the crowd, making Carter forget all about his earlier nerves. He lost himself in the moment, the guitar in his hands becoming an extension of his body as his muscle memory took over and he played without conscious thought.

He turned back to the audience and stepped forward to the mic, ready to start singing. But just as he opened his mouth, motion at the front of the bar drew his eye.

The door was swinging shut behind a woman who had just stepped inside. A woman with red hair and delicate features. A woman he'd spent the last year and a half dreaming about.

Sophia.

She was back.

Sophia saw him immediately. He was standing on the stage at the far end of the bar, and based on the music, he and the guys had just started to play.

Their eyes met across the crowd. An electric shock zinged through her and she felt a tug in the area of her belly button. She took a step forward, unable to resist the pull of attraction, the need to get closer to him.

After all this time, Sophia hadn't expected Carter to affect her so strongly. She was a different person now; becoming a mother had transformed her in ways she was still exploring. But none of that seemed to matter now that she'd seen him again.

He opened his mouth and started to sing. She closed her eyes as his voice washed over her, the sound deep and smooth, with the slightest hint of a rasp that scraped along her nerve endings and made her shiver.

She took a long breath, and suddenly she was back in Hank's office, her body pressed against Carter's chest as he touched her, kissed her. Filled her. She recalled the feel of his palm as it cupped her breast, the gentle scrape of his calluses across her sensitive skin. The soap-sage scent of him growing stronger as heat flared between them. And the taste of him in her mouth, that warm spice that was more intoxicating than any drug.

Her legs shook with the memory, and she searched for a chair. The place was full, but there was a small spot by the bar where she could wait.

She gingerly sat on the rickety bar stool, holding her breath for a second as she waited to see if it would collapse. So far, so good.

"Well, well, well."

She turned to find Hank standing across the bar,

his eyebrows raised as he looked at her. "The prodigal bartender returns."

Sophia smiled at him. "It's good to see you, too, Hank."

"Didn't say that," he replied gruffly. He set a half-pint glass in front of her, brimming with just the right amount of froth.

She reached into her purse, grabbed a bill and set it on the bar.

Hank shook his head. "No charge. This time," he added.

Sophia nodded, returning her money to her wallet. "Thanks." She raised her glass and toasted him. "Cheers."

"How long are you in town for?"

Her glance slid to the stage. She felt another zing when she saw that Carter was staring at her. Was he going to watch her like this for his whole set? Warmth bloomed in her chest at the thought. It was nice to know she wasn't the only one feeling caught off guard at the moment.

"I'm not sure," she said, keeping her eyes on the man she'd come to see. "That depends on a few things." Like how Carter responded to the news he was a father.

The thought of telling him felt like a glass of cold water had been thrown over her growing arousal. She didn't come here to flirt or to pick up where they'd left off all that time ago. She had some important, life-changing news to deliver. And while she was glad to still feel a connection to Carter, she didn't dare hope it would remain after she dropped her bombshell.

"Well, if you're looking for something to do, I could always use the help."

She looked away from Carter and glanced back at Hank. "I appreciate that," she said. "But I have my hands full right now." Between inventorying the house, taking care of Ben and stressing about what to say to Carter, she was swamped.

Hank shrugged. "Offer stands," he said. He gave her a nod and moved away to serve another customer.

She smiled, though he couldn't see her. Hank had a gruff exterior, but despite his grumbling, he had a kind heart.

The guys launched into another song. She leaned back and watched, sipping her beer as the music washed over her. Danny caught her eye and nodded with a grin. She lifted her glass slightly in acknowledgment. He'd been the one to let her know they were playing tonight.

"I know it's a long shot, but this will be his first show after the accident. We'd love to see you," he'd said.

"Actually, I should be able to make it." She'd briefly explained about Will and the house, conveniently leaving out the part about Ben and her real need to see Carter. Better for Danny and James to think she was stopping by out of friendly interest. If Carter wanted them to know about Ben, he could share the news in his own time and on his own terms.

She'd sent Carter a few get-well cards since his accident. Had even considered giving him her phone number. But every time she went to add it to one of the cards, her hand refused to write the numbers. She'd known that if he called her, she wouldn't be able to keep Ben's existence a secret any longer. And this was not a conversation she wanted to have over the phone. Some news needed to be delivered in person.

"Hey, girl." Sadie, one of the waitresses, touched her arm. "Haven't seen you in a minute."

Sophia hopped off the stool and hugged the other woman. "It's good to see you! How've you been?"

Sadie blew a tuft of hair off her forehead. "Oh, you know. Staying busy."

"Keeps you out of trouble."

The young woman gave her a sly grin. "I don't know about that."

"Just be careful," Sophia cautioned. Sadie was a bit of a wild child, something Sophia had envied a little back when they'd worked together.

"You sound like my mom," Sadie said, shaking her head. "Anyway, you want some food? I could bring you a burger or something." She wrinkled her nose and leaned in close. "Stay away from the nachos," she said, voice pitched low. "The chips are really stale."

"Thanks, but I'm good," Sophia said. She probably should eat, so she wouldn't be drinking on an empty stomach, but just the thought of food made her queasy. She was already nervous about talking to Carter. A greasy burger was the last thing she needed right now.

"Holler if you change your mind," Sadie said before flouncing away. Sophia turned back to the stage in time to see the guys wrap up another song. She expected them to launch into the next one, but instead Carter leaned into the mic.

"If it's okay with you folks, we're gonna take a little break." He said it to the crowd, but since he was looking directly at her, Sophia knew he was really talking to her.

Nerves flared to life in her stomach as she watched him set down his guitar. He picked up his cane and navigated the stairs carefully. A small shock went through her at this obvious reminder of his accident. Up on the stage, he'd looked larger than life and just as he had been. But now, seeing his measured gait gave her a deeper understanding of just how badly he'd been hurt.

Doubt surged in her chest. Was this the right time to tell him about Ben? What if he wasn't strong enough to handle the news yet? Should she wait a few more months? It wasn't like her baby was going anywhere— she could always share this information later.

But as Carter approached, she saw the glint of determination in his eyes. No, she couldn't put this off any longer. She could always come up with an excuse not to tell him about his son. There would never be a perfect time to hear the news. And the longer she waited, the more unfair it was to Ben. If Carter wanted to be his dad, she couldn't in good conscience deprive her son of his presence any longer.

Her mind spun as Carter drew near, taking in the well-wishes of the crowd as he walked. Someone pulled him aside, halting his progress so they could chatter in his ear. She'd practiced this meeting in her mind a thousand times, but now that she was actually in the moment, all her carefully rehearsed words flew out of her brain. Her heart ached as she pictured Ben, asleep in his crib, little hands curled and mouth slack, his body totally relaxed. Leah was watching over him while she was here. Would Carter love him the way she did?

Was she making a huge mistake?

The pressure built inside her, and she knew something had to give. Sophia felt split, cleaved in two by her warring desires.

To protect her son.

To make sure her son knew his father.

There were no easy answers here. She'd thought seeing Carter would help her relax, that his presence would reassure her that he was a good guy. Instead, coming here had stirred up conflicting emotions that made her even more agitated. Her body wanted him again. What she wouldn't give to be able to pick up where they'd left off! But her heart wasn't about to forget the baby sleeping at home. She had to do right by him, even if it hurt.

It's going to be okay, she told herself. *He's still the same Carter I knew.*

But was he? The last year and a half had irrevocably changed her. Given the severity of his accident, it stood to reason he'd changed, too.

I can do this.

Even as she formed the thought, doubt crept in, fraying the edges of her conviction.

Carter was still several feet away, nearly surrounded by people wanting to talk to him. Sophia glanced at the bar, looking for her drink. Water would be better, but right now she'd settle for anything wet to help drown her nerves.

She took a sip, swallowed and winced.

Get it together, she chided herself. She'd come here to talk to him. To reconnect and ask him to stop by the house tomorrow. That was when the really tough conversation would take place, when he'd learn he was a father. This was going to be nothing more than a friendly chat.

She turned back to the crowd, wanting to know how much time she had left in this "before" part of her life.

The answer was staring her in the face.

None. The time was now.

Carter was standing right in front of her.

Chapter 5

She's really here.

When Carter had first seen Sophia walk into the bar, part of him had wondered if his eyes were playing tricks on him. He'd always hoped to see her again, but never in his wildest dreams had he ever imagined she would come here to see him play his first show in what seemed like forever.

He tried to think of something clever to say, but his thoughts were a jumble, making it difficult to pick out words.

"You're back."

She smiled, looking a little nervous. "So are you." She nodded at the stage. "I'm glad to see you're okay after what happened. You sound good up there. How does it feel to be playing again?"

"Exhilarating," he replied. "And terrifying," he added. "But it was time. I needed to have something in my life that didn't change."

A shadow crossed her face. "I can understand that," she said. "The desire to go back to when life seemed simple."

She was quiet for a moment, and Carter wondered what she was thinking about. Had something happened to her in El Paso? Was graduate school not what she'd thought it was going to be?

He took a step forward, wanting to touch her. But he stopped himself from making the gesture. They hadn't seen each other in a year and a half. And while she'd once welcomed his touch, she might not any longer.

"I didn't know you were back in Alpine," he said, changing the topic. "What brought you to town?"

"It's kind of a long story," she began. She looked past him to the stage. "I don't want to hold you up, but to make a long story short, one of the regulars at the bar died recently, and to my shock, he left me his house and everything in it."

Carter felt his eyes widen. "Seriously?"

She nodded. "Yeah." She looked like she didn't quite believe it herself. "I had no idea Will was even thinking about making me his beneficiary."

"Oh, I remember Will." The image of the older man's face flashed across Carter's mind. He'd always been friendly and had bought the band a few rounds on occasion. Carter remembered watching him bend Sophia's ear many times while he and the guys were playing. She'd always been a good sport about listening to him, and Carter had known from the look on Will's face that he was taken with her.

Not that he'd blamed the older man. Carter had been quite taken with her himself.

Still was, in fact.

He watched her face as she described the house and all the stuff inside. She'd changed since moving to El Paso; she'd cut her hair, the red strands now falling just below her chin rather than past her shoulders. There were a few faint lines at the corners of her eyes, evidence of the stress of her graduate studies. And while her brown eyes were still full of warmth, there was a hint of wariness there, as though she wasn't quite sure about something.

She looked good, though. He'd spent the first set checking her out, playing with only half a brain. Even though there had been a fair bit of distance between them, Carter could swear she seemed curvier than he remembered. And now that he was close, he was convinced his impressions were correct—her breasts and hips *were* a bit fuller than the last time he'd seen her. He had the sudden urge to pull her into his arms and press her body against his, to feel her softness once more.

"—come by?"

He caught the rising inflection in her voice and realized she was asking him a question. He shook his head, tuning back in to the conversation once more. "Sorry, I didn't catch that." He pointed to his ear, pretending the noise of the bar had interfered with his hearing. It was either that or admit he'd been distracted by thoughts of touching her…

Sophia nodded and leaned closer. A lesser man might have taken the opportunity to glance down her shirt, but Carter thought of himself as a gentleman, and so kept his eyes firmly on her face.

"I was hoping you might stop by tomorrow," Sophia said. They were so close he could see the flecks of gold in her brown eyes, an accent that was almost hypnotizing.

Carter found himself nodding before she'd even finished asking the question. "I'd like that," he said. It was too hard to talk here, with all the noise and the people. It would be far easier to converse in the peace and quiet of her new home. And if catching up led to something a little more…physical? Well, the privacy would be the icing on the cake.

Sophia gave him the address. Not trusting his memory, he typed it into his phone, then added her number, as well.

"What time should I stop by?"

"How about one?" she suggested. "I'll fix us something for lunch and we can talk."

"Perfect." Margot was meeting Mike for a lunch date at twelve thirty. Carter could drop her off at the restaurant and then head to Sophia's. He wasn't supposed to drive long distances by himself, but a trip across town shouldn't be an issue. "What can I bring?"

"Potato chips, I guess?" she suggested. "I wasn't

planning on fixing anything too fancy—just sandwiches and a salad."

"That sounds great. You know I'm easy to please."
He grinned at her, his mind already drifting to the
idea of dessert...

"Yes, I seem to remember that," she murmured.
Heat flared in her eyes, making his stomach do a little flip in his belly.

Well.

Seemed he *wasn't* the only one who remembered
their last meeting.

Warmth spread from the center of his chest down
his limbs, causing his skin to tingle. He hadn't intended to bring up their encounter; he wasn't sure
how Sophia would respond, and he hadn't wanted to
make her feel uncomfortable. But apparently it was
on her mind.

And that was just fine with him.

He dropped his gaze to her mouth. The tip of her
tongue darted out, moistening her lips. He smiled,
recognizing an invitation when he saw one.

Carter dipped his head, then gazed into her eyes
before he closed the distance between them. Sophia's
expression was one of desire and anticipation mixed
with intense longing.

Her reaction ignited his own smoldering arousal,
sparking a flame of need that clouded his judgment.
Hank's office was just a few feet away. They could
sneak inside and lock the door and pick up where
they'd left off with no one the wiser.

In the dim recesses of his brain, he realized that

everyone would, in fact, know what they were doing, and that Hank would not be cool with them using his office as their own personal love shack. But right now, with Sophia so close they were breathing the same air, Carter just didn't care.

Part of him wanted to prolong this moment, to draw out the delicious anticipation sparking between them. But the other, louder part of his body screamed at him to kiss her already.

He took one last look at her face, her eyes shining with need. Then he leaned down and brushed his mouth over hers.

The first thing he registered was her warmth. It came as a bit of a shock; he hadn't kissed a woman since she'd left, so he'd nearly forgotten what it was like to have warm, supple lips pressed against his own. It was a heady sensation, one that he could drown in if he dared to let go.

Carter brought his hand to Sophia's jaw, his fingertips brushing against the strands of hair tucked behind her ear. He could feel the pulse thrumming in her neck, a galloping beat that matched the pace of his own heart. She placed her palm high on his chest, her touch as hot as a brand even though the fabric of his shirt kept their skin from touching.

Her lips parted and he slipped his tongue inside her mouth. He tasted the faint tang of the beer she'd been drinking. Her fingers dug into his chest as she tightened her grip on his shirt.

Carter moved his other hand to her lower back, pulling her forward until she was pressed against him.

The curves of her breasts and the soft roundness of her belly fit against him perfectly. The blood thundered in his ears at it raced south, his body instinctively responding to the feel of Sophia in his arms.

He wasn't sure how long they stayed together. Seconds? Hours? It didn't matter. Time ceased to exist for him. His awareness shrank, making it seem like he and Sophia were the only two people in the world.

Carter tilted his head, changing the angle of the kiss. It was at that moment a loud twang rang through the bar. He and Sophia both jumped at the sudden intrusion, breaking their connection. She stared up at him for a few dazed seconds, her skin flushed and her lips shiny. His confusion was mirrored in her eyes, both of them breathing hard as they tried to regain equilibrium.

An electric-guitar version of "Here Comes the Bride" started up, and Carter turned toward the stage to find James and Danny watching him, the pair wearing identical sly grins. He shot them a glare, which only made them laugh.

He turned back to Sophia with an apologetic shrug. "Sorry about them," he said, running a hand through his hair. "I can't take 'em anywhere."

A faint smile tugged at the corners of her mouth. "It's fine," she murmured, giving the pair in question a little wave. "They just like to tease you."

She returned her focus to Carter. "Well…" For a moment, neither one of them spoke. He wasn't sure what to say in the face of that amazing kiss. *Please stay? Let's go home together?* Both phrases sounded too desperate. He wasn't trying to play hard to get, but he didn't want her to think he was only interested in getting into her pants again.

"Tomorrow?" he asked. It hadn't taken long to re-ignite the chemistry he'd always felt with Sophia. Hopefully tomorrow they'd have more time and privacy to explore that connection.

She nodded. "Yes. I'll see you then." She picked up her bag and headed for the door.

Carter stayed rooted to the spot, watching her hips sway as she moved. What was it about this woman that got under his skin? She was beautiful, but not in a knockout-model kind of way, and she wasn't what society would call thin. And, yeah, she was smart, but not intimidatingly so. Any other man would look at her and see an average woman. But in Carter's eyes, she was damn near perfect.

Sophia paused at the door and turned around for one last look. She glanced at the stage first, but when she didn't find him there, she looked back at the bar. He gave her a little wave, and she smiled.

Tomorrow, he mouthed.

She nodded and winked at him. Then she walked out the door.

Carter stood there for a second, wanting to follow her. But as Danny added a drum solo to James's guitar, he knew he couldn't bail on his friends. So he turned and headed back toward the stage, enduring the winks and knowing grins from the crowd as he moved past.

"Somebody was glad to see you," Danny said as Carter picked up his guitar.

Carter just shook his head, hoping the guys would drop it.

"You gonna be able to play?" James teased. "For a minute there, I thought we were gonna need to hit you two with the hose to get you apart."

"Very funny," Carter said. "I'm ready to go. What do you want to play?"

His buddies exchanged a look. "How about 'You Shook Me All Night Long'?" Danny suggested.

Carter shot him a dirty look, but it was too late. James and Danny started playing the intro, and he had no choice but to step up to the mic and sing.

As he launched into the first lines of the song, he realized his bandmates had known all along that Sophia would be here tonight. Danny's earlier friendly-face remark now made perfect sense.

He wanted to be mad at the guys, but he just couldn't dredge up the emotion. Even though he'd never talked about his attraction to Sophia, Danny and James had both remarked on it before she'd moved away. In fact, both of them had encouraged him to ask her out. Was this their way of helping him so he didn't miss his shot? Not everyone got a second chance. It seemed like his friends had pulled a few strings to make sure he did.

And this time, he intended to take advantage of it.

The next morning was clear and warm, so much so that Sophia had to blast the air conditioner in her car to keep from melting into a puddle. Texas summers were brutal, and August was pretty much the worst month of the year when it came to heat.

She reviewed her mental to-do list as she drove home from the supermarket. Unload the groceries, play with Ben, feed him lunch, put him down for a nap, then make the sandwiches and salad for her lunch with Carter. Hopefully Ben's pattern of a two-hour nap would hold and she'd have time to talk to Carter before springing his son on him. She still wasn't sure what, exactly, she was going to say to him, but she wanted to ease into the subject while they ate, then save the introductions for after Carter had had a little time to adjust to the shock.

"Like a few minutes is going to make a difference," she muttered to herself. This was going to be hard no matter how much she tried to soften the blow before breaking the news.

And adding to the difficulty? The knowledge that the chemistry between her and Carter was still off the charts.

Last night's kiss had been completely unexpected. Sophia had figured she'd go to Hank's, watch Carter and the guys play and have a friendly chat with him between sets. Not even in her wildest dreams had she imagined Carter would react so strongly to seeing her again.

Not that it had been one-sided. Her hormones had woken up the second she'd laid eyes on him. When he'd touched her, she'd nearly jumped into his arms right there in the middle of the bar. There was no doubt in her mind that if they'd been somewhere more private, they wouldn't have stopped at just a kiss.

She reached for the dashboard and cranked up the fan a little more. Just thinking about him sent a flush over her body.

"Get it together," she told herself. The minireunion with Carter had been nice, but she had more important things to think about now.

Sophia glanced in her rearview mirror, smiling at Ben's reflection. He was turned around, facing the back of the car, and so she had placed a mirror on the back of the rear seat so he would have something to look at. It also made it so she could keep an eye on him while she drove. Seeing him frown now, she pressed a button on the small remote mounted to her sun visor. Ben's mirror transformed into a blinking light display, complete with a catchy tune. The baby grinned as the program started and he displayed his two bottom teeth to great effect.

His dimples reminded her of Carter's grin last night, when he'd flashed his own set at her. Even though she'd never seen baby pictures of Carter, she was willing to bet Ben was the spitting image of his father at that age.

She turned onto the quiet street where Will's house was located. Although technically it was her house now, Sophia had a hard time thinking of it as such. It would always be Will's place, as far as she was concerned, and that was fine since she wasn't planning on living here long anyway.

It's pretty enough, she thought as she approached

the driveway. A little on the older side, but Will had done a good job maintaining it, so the place had aged well. The brick was a dark tan color and the trim was painted a sage green that blended well with the desert environment. Will hadn't bothered with grass in the yard; instead, he'd elected to use native plants and a liberal amount of rocks to create curb appeal. It had been a smart decision, she realized now. No lawn to mow, and very little watering required.

That'll be a good selling point.

The inside of the house was also in decent shape. The walls could do with a fresh coat of paint, and the carpet could stand to be cleaned. But overall, Will had taken good care of his home. He really had left her a gift, and while Sophia still didn't understand why he'd chosen her, she was grateful to him. The sale of his home and belongings would make her life much easier from a financial perspective. She'd be able to give Ben every opportunity to learn and grow and thrive, without having to worry about finding the money to pay for it. Will didn't know it, but his actions would ensure her son had everything he needed and more. It was a relief to know that if Carter decided he didn't want to be a part of Ben's life, Sophia would still be able to afford to provide for her baby.

She pulled into the garage and cut the engine. Her first order of business was getting Ben out of the car—it was far too warm to leave him in the back seat while she unloaded the groceries. As soon as she put him in the playpen in the living room, he started to protest. She grabbed a toy from the counter and offered it to him. It was a simple plastic egg filled with beans that rattled at the slightest movement. Ben liked to feel the vibrations of the beans as he shook the egg, which bought Sophia a few minutes to get the bags of food into the house. She was just starting to put things away when the doorbell rang.

She glanced at the clock and frowned. Surely that wasn't Carter? He didn't seem like the type to show up two hours early. But maybe he was so eager to see her again he couldn't wait?

Sophia bit her bottom lip and pressed a hand to her stomach, which currently felt like home to a thousand butterflies. She'd really wanted Ben to be asleep when Carter arrived so he wouldn't see him right away, but apparently that wasn't going to happen. For a split second, she considered not answering the door. But then she shook her head—she might as well get this over with.

Ben grinned up at her as she walked past the playpen, his fists clenched around his toy.

"I love you," she said, signing as she spoke.

Ben responded by taking one hand and placing his fingers on his chin—his baby version of saying *Mama*.

She smiled. "Yes, Mama loves you." She echoed his sign with the adult form, her fingers spread wide as she tapped her chin with her thumb.

She took a deep breath as she approached the door. *Here we go*, she thought.

A man stood on the porch, his face shadowed by the curved brim of a worn ball cap. He had deep-set brown eyes, a thin nose and a scraggly crop of stubble on his cheeks and chin.

Sophia blinked, taken aback by his presence. "Um, can I help you?"

He jerked the hat off his head, revealing a mop of dirty blond strands that looked like they hadn't seen a comb in a long time. "Yeah. I'm looking for my grandpa. He lives here." He shifted as he spoke, his gaze going past her to the interior of the house, as if he expected someone to join her at the door.

"What's your grandfather's name?" Apprehension rose in Sophia's chest as she waited for his response.

"William Porter. But everyone calls him Will."

Sophia's heart dropped as her suspicions were confirmed. "I'm sorry to have to be the one to tell you this, but Will passed away a few months ago."

The young man's eyes widened. "What? That's not possible. Someone would have told me."

"What's your name?" Sophia's mind raced as she studied the stranger, looking for any hint of Will's features in his face.

The attorney had told her Will had no surviving family, which was why he'd left everything to her. Either the lawyer had been wrong, or this guy was trying to pull a con.

"Jake. Porter," he added hastily. His eyes kept darting past her, into the house. There was something slightly predatory about his demeanor, an air about him that made the hair on the back of Sophia's neck stand on end.

"Well, Jake, I'm sorry for your loss." She started

to shut the door, but his hand shot out, pressing flat against the wood to keep it open.

Sophia's heart jumped into her throat. "What do you think you're doing?" Her voice didn't waver, but her knees started shaking. She had no weapons in the house and nothing close to hand that could be used to keep this man out. If he wanted to come inside, there wasn't much she would be able to do to stop him.

"Who are you? Why are you in his house?" There was a heavy dose of accusation in his voice; it was clear he thought she didn't belong here.

"I bought it," she lied, dodging the question about her name. No way was she going to explain the inheritance issue to him. "Now, if you'll excuse me, my husband will be home soon."

Surprise flashed across Jake's face, and he removed his hand. "I'm sorry," he said. "I didn't mean to scare you."

Her first instinct was to accept his apology, but Sophia's heart was still pounding. "I'm sorry I can't help you," she said. She shut the door and flipped the lock into place with shaking fingers. Then she raced into the living room and scooped up Ben. Grabbing her phone, she stood by the door to the garage and waited, wondering if she was going to have to load her baby into the car and flee, or if Jake would leave.

She heard muffled cursing, then a loud thump as though Jake had kicked the wall. Sophia's thumb hovered over the numbers on her phone screen. Should she call the police? What could they even do? It wasn't like the man had overtly threatened her—he'd simply scared her.

The seconds ticked by as she waited to see what he'd do next. *Just leave*, she thought, over and over again.

After what seemed like an eternity, she heard his footsteps on the path outside, then the faint sound of a car door slamming. An engine turned over in the driveway, and after a few seconds, the noise faded as Jake drove away.

Still trembling, Sophia returned to the living room and sat down with Ben. He immediately took off, crawling over to a small collection of toys on the floor. He played happily, oblivious to her fear. That was good, at least.

Her mind whirled as she considered her options. It seemed like overkill to call the police now that Jake was gone. And he hadn't consciously intimidated her. But there was something about the man that seemed…off. She definitely didn't trust his claim that he was Will's grandson. In all the times they'd spoken, Will had never mentioned grandchildren. She knew he'd had a son, but the man had died years ago. Sophia had never pressed him for more information, as just the mention of his son's name had been enough to make the old guy tear up.

Now that she had a child of her own, she completely understood his reaction.

Given Will's grief over his son, Sophia figured he would have mentioned it if he'd left any children behind. His silence on the subject wasn't definitive proof, but given what the lawyer had told her, she was inclined to think Jake was lying.

Still, best to be sure. She dialed the number for the attorney's office. His secretary answered on the second ring and gave the standard he's-in-a-meeting line. Sophia left a detailed message explaining what had just happened, including a description of Jake. Hopefully the woman on the other end of the line didn't leave anything out.

"I'll let him know, Ms. Burns."

"Thanks," Sophia replied, hoping the secretary would at least put her message on top of the pile.

She set the phone on the table and watched her baby boy play, feeling her body relax as the adrenaline faded from her system. Ben's current favorite toy was a bulky dump truck that rumbled with flashing lights when he pushed a button. He sat a few feet away, pressing the button and laughing at the display.

Sophia smiled at the sight, happy to know he was adjusting well to their new routine. She'd worried that taking him out of El Paso and away from everything familiar would be hard for him, but he was taking things like a champ.

He took a break from his dump truck to rub his eyes with small fists. With a start, Sophia glanced at her phone. She cursed softly, even though Ben couldn't hear.

Carter would be here soon. She needed to get started on lunch.

Moving quickly, she finished putting things away in the kitchen. Then she scooped up Ben and wrestled him into a clean diaper. It was time for his nap, and given his rapidly declining mood, he was ready for it.

She settled into the rocking chair in the corner of the dim bedroom. This was one moment she refused to rush. Rocking her baby was one of the highlights of her day, especially since he was growing more independent by the hour. In the back of her mind, she knew that someday soon he wouldn't let her hold him, wouldn't have time for her snuggles. She was determined to enjoy this while she still could.

Ben's body relaxed as she rocked, and he reached up to rest one little hand in the hollow of her throat. Knowing what he wanted, Sophia began to sing.

After a few minutes, his eyelids began to droop. Sophia knew she should transfer him into the portable crib so he could fall asleep on his own, but she couldn't bring herself to let go of him just yet. He was so precious, so perfect to her. And within an hour, his father might decide to reject him.

"I will take care of you, my love," she said, tracing the line of his eyebrows with her fingertip. "No matter what happens, I'll always be here."

Sophia knew what it was like to grow up without a father. It wasn't something she'd ever wanted for her own children. If Carter walked away, she'd do her best to find another man who would care for Ben as much as she did. It wouldn't be easy, but she was ready to do whatever it took to make sure her baby had a loving man in his life.

Don't get ahead of yourself, she thought. Ever since Ben's birth, Sophia had been mentally preparing herself for Carter to turn his back on the baby. It was part of her personality—to plan for the worst—but she had to keep reminding herself that Carter didn't know about Ben. He hadn't been given a chance to respond yet. She had to stop assuming he would reject his son. Things could just as easily work out for the best.

She carefully rose from the rocking chair and stepped over to the portable crib. After pressing a soft kiss to Ben's forehead, she placed her sleeping baby on the mattress.

"He's going to love you," she said, whispering even though her voice wouldn't disturb his slumber.

She had to believe it was true. The alternative would simply break her heart.

Jake pulled off to the side of the road, too keyed up to drive safely.

Dead. The old man was dead.

He didn't want to believe it. Didn't want to accept that his grandfather was really gone. Why hadn't anyone told him? Why had he found out from a stranger living in his grandfather's house?

And just who was she, anyway? She'd seemed nervous when he had mentioned his grandfather's name. Like she didn't want to talk about him. But if she'd never met the old man before, if she'd simply bought the house after he'd died, why would she care?

He shook his head, trying to organize his thoughts. There was something off about the situation. When he'd looked past her shoulder into the house, he'd recognized his grandfather's furniture and other things.

Why was all of that still inside? It should have been cleared out after his death.

"It should have gone to me," he muttered to himself.

The house, its contents. All the money the old man had in his accounts. He should have inherited it all.

Instead, he was sitting behind the wheel of a rental while some woman lived large in his grandfather's home, enjoying his things.

No, not her things. My things.

By rights, all of that was his. She had no claim to any of it.

He thought back over their conversation, if such a brief interaction qualified as such. She'd been pretty enough; hair too red for his liking, but her big brown eyes made up for it. Seemed like she had a nice rack under the boring T-shirt.

An idea began to form in his mind. Jake had never known his grandmother—she'd died before he was born. Grandpa had lived alone for what seemed like forever. It stood to reason he'd been lonely. An easy mark for a woman like her—chat him up, act nice and friendly. Get him on the hook. He'd fall for her, ask her to move in. She'd make him feel loved, tell him he was her soul mate. Talk him into changing his will and leaving her everything. All she had to do was pretend to care until he died.

Yes, he thought, nodding. That was probably exactly what had happened. She was some grifter who'd spied a lonely old man and decided to take advantage of him. No wonder she'd seemed scared at the mention of his grandfather. Now that Jake was back in town, her scheme was at risk of being exposed.

Had he even died of natural causes? Or had she hastened things along once Grandpa had signed his will to ensure he didn't have a chance to change his mind?

Anger filled Jake's chest as he pictured her serving Will a meal, all smiles as she watched him eat food she'd laced with medication. Old people died every day. No one would question it as long as it looked like a natural death.

"Bitch," he muttered. She thought she'd gotten away with it. But Jake knew a con when he saw one. He wasn't about to sit back and let her take everything that was his.

He threw the truck into gear and jerked back onto the road. The tires squealed in protest as he pulled a tight U-turn.

Her time was up. He was going back there, and he wasn't going to let her lies about a husband coming home soon scare him away again.

The engine revved as he stepped on the gas. At the house on the corner, a woman stood on her porch watering flowers. She yelled something at him as he sped past, probably admonishing him to slow down. Jake didn't care. How many of these neighbors had stood by while this woman had taken advantage of his grandfather, swindling Jake out of his inheritance?

There was a truck in front of him, its pace maddeningly slow. Jake rode up on the bumper, hoping to encourage the guy to go a little faster. If anything, the driver slowed even more.

Grinding his teeth, Jake eased off the gas. He was just a few houses away—he'd have to brake soon anyway.

To his shock, the truck in front of him tapped the brakes and turned into the driveway of his grandfather's house. Jake immediately pulled over, wanting to get a look at this new visitor. He cut the engine and pretended to dig for something in the passenger seat, trying to look like he belonged in the neighborhood.

A man slowly climbed down from the driver's seat. He moved awkwardly, as though he was in pain. Once his feet were on the ground, he reached into the truck and withdrew a cane, then a bouquet of flowers.

Jake frowned as he watched the scene unfold. The guy didn't look old—why was he hobbling around with a cane?

The man ambled up the walk, flowers in hand. Jake couldn't see the porch or door from this angle, so he waited a few minutes, wanting to give the man enough time to get inside. When he was sure the coast was clear, he started the truck again and began to inch forward.

Interesting. Maybe she wasn't lying about the husband after all. Were they a team, working together to scam people? She took on the older men, while he ran cons on the older ladies? Or was he going to be her latest victim?

He didn't look very tough. Jake could probably take him on in a fight, if it came to that. He could stop right now, bang on the door and demand answers. Whoever the man was, he wouldn't be able to prevent Jake from coming inside.

It was a tempting thought. The woman was still probably a little shaken by his visit. That gave him the advantage. If he waited, she'd have time to recover, time to practice her lies so they sounded more convincing.

But on the other hand, if he waited, that gave him time, too. He could do a little investigating, find out exactly who she was and when she'd come into his grandfather's life. Then he could prove without a shadow of a doubt that she didn't belong here, didn't deserve to live in the house. It shouldn't take long.

He rolled past the house, righteous anger building inside him. Every moment this interloper remained in his house kept him from the tables. He needed to get her out, sell the house and everything inside, and take the money back to Vegas so he could get back on top again.

"Enjoy it while you can," he snarled. "You won't have it much longer."

Chapter 6

Carter stood on the welcome mat, feeling surprisingly nervous at the prospect of seeing Sophia again. Last night at the bar, things had seemed surreal. He'd woken this morning and been half-convinced it had all been a dream—seeing her, holding her. Kissing her. It was all too perfect, a manifestation of his fantasies over the last several months. But then he'd checked his phone and found the note to himself with her address and number.

Definitely *not* a dream.

He'd wanted to rush over as soon as he'd stepped out of the shower, to hopefully pick up where they'd left off last night. But he'd forced himself to slow down and had dug deep for patience. Sophia would not ap-

preciate him arriving so early, and besides, he had to
drop Margot off at the café for her lunch with Mike.

His sister's excitement had been a nice distraction,
kept him from obsessing over his own upcoming date.

"You look nice," he'd told her.

Margot had smiled, done a little twirl in the kitchen
to make the skirt of her dress flare. She'd put on
makeup and pulled back her hair with a beaded bar-
rette. It was a nice change from her usual, practical
wardrobe, and it was clear she was enjoying the excuse to dress up a bit.

Do you think I'm overdressed? she'd asked.

Not at all.

They'd arrived at the café a few minutes early. It
didn't matter, though; Mike was already there, standing out front. He'd looked sharp in a pair of khakis, a
button-down shirt and a tweed sport coat. Carter was
pleased to see he'd dressed up for his sister—it was
another small sign of Mike's regard for her.

Margot would have jumped out of the truck right
away, but Carter had held her back for a second.

Let me know when you need me to get you, he'd
said. *And if you feel uncomfortable at all—*

I know, I know, she'd interrupted impatiently. *I'll
text you. Don't worry about me. Go have fun on your
own date.*

She'd left then, without so much as a backward
glance in his direction. Carter had waited a second,
wanting to see Mike's reaction when he saw Margot.

He hadn't disappointed. A flash of pleasure had
lit his features and he'd smiled broadly as Margot

approached. He'd stepped forward to meet her, his hands already moving to sign a greeting.

Good, Carter had thought. Objectively, he knew Margot was an adult. She lived on her own, worked a job she enjoyed, went out with friends on a regular basis. Hell, maybe she even explored the dating scene in Austin. Logically, Carter understood she didn't need him looking out for her. But she was still his little sister. And he would always worry about her, especially when she was in a situation where he knew she was the only Deaf person.

Now, though, he had his own issues to worry about.

He took a deep breath and reached out to press the doorbell. Excitement and nervousness swirled in his belly, an unsettling combination. He wanted to know all about Sophia's life in El Paso and her graduate studies. Too bad he didn't have anything interesting to tell her in return. His life had been dominated by medical procedures and therapy. Not exactly scintillating conversation.

Maybe we won't need to talk, whispered a small voice inside his head. Carter hadn't had any romantic experiences since that night at the bar with Sophia. He'd probably have to make some adjustments to accommodate his still-healing body, but if Sophia was interested, he was damn sure willing to experiment.

Before that thought could develop further, the door opened. Sophia offered him a smile. "Hey. Come in."

She looked even better in the daylight, if such a thing was possible. Her brown eyes were clear and warm, and her hair was tucked behind her ears. She had a fresh-faced, girl-next-door look about her today. It was clear she wasn't trying to be sexy, but in Carter's eyes, her casual appearance was a potent aphrodisiac.

He smiled and stepped inside, catching a whiff of her floral-scented shampoo as he moved past. "These are for you," he said, handing her the bouquet.

It was a simple arrangement—carnations and daisies. But he'd liked the colors and he hadn't wanted to arrive empty-handed.

Sophia beamed as she took them. "Thanks," she said, holding them to her nose and taking a sniff. "They're lovely."

It was then Carter realized he was supposed to bring something else. "Oh, damn," he muttered to himself.

"What's wrong?"

He shook his head, feeling foolish. "You asked me to bring chips. I totally forgot."

She grinned at him. "Don't worry about it. We'll do just fine without them. Probably healthier, anyway." She touched his arm as she walked by. "Come into the kitchen with me. I want to get these in some water."

He propped his cane against the wall and followed her down a short hall, checking things out as they walked. It seemed like a nice home. The formal dining room was just off the hallway, in the front of the house. He spied a large round table and a matching china hutch through the door as they moved past. The living room was to the right—a large, carpeted expanse lined with bookshelves. The sofa looked a little flat, but from what he could see, the upholstery was clean, if a bit faded.

The kitchen was long, with the refrigerator and oven opposite each other at one end of the room. The linoleum counters and cabinets were the color of a ripe avocado, and the walls sported a mandala-patterned paper that he couldn't bring himself to stare at directly.

"Whoa," he said, drawing up short in the face of all that green.

Sophia laughed as she opened up cabinets in her search for a vase. "I know. It's a bit much. Wait until you see the bathroom. The toilet is pink."

"Seriously?"

She nodded. "I have a feeling Will let his wife have free rein when it came to decorating the house. I'm guessing after she was gone, he couldn't bear to change anything."

Carter felt a pang of sympathy for the old man, imagining him rattling around these rooms, surrounded by reminders of his wife.

"Well, the good news is I hear the vintage look is coming back."

Sophia found a vase on the top shelf of one of the cabinets. "This definitely qualifies." She stood on her toes, but couldn't quite reach it.

Carter walked over and grabbed it for her. Their bodies brushed as he brought down his arm, but she didn't move away.

He captured her gaze for a moment, holding the

vase between them. The silence grew heavy, seemed almost electrically charged as the seconds ticked by. Possibilities stretched before them. Should he kiss her? Or would that be too presumptuous?

A sudden rattle made them both jump. A gust of cold air blasted the top of Carter's head as the air-conditioning kicked on. They smiled at each other, and he handed her the vase. "Here you go."

"Thanks," she said, sounding a little shy. She arranged the flowers to her liking and set them on the counter. "Are you hungry?"

It was an innocent question, but Carter's libido perked up. "Yes," he replied. *In more ways than one.*

Sophia nodded. "I thought we might eat in the dining room. It's a little less…distracting." She waved her hand to encompass the wallpaper, counters and cabinets. The kitchen decor had likely been the height of sophistication back in the day, but now the swirling patterns and overwhelming blast of bright colors made Carter feel anxious.

"That sounds perfect. How can I help?"

"Bring the flowers," she said, handing him the vase. "I've already made the food. I'll meet you in the dining room."

He did as he was told, carrying his cargo down the hall. Closer inspection of the dining room revealed gold-and-cream paper on the walls and a butter-yellow carpet. Not his first choice of colors, but a lot more subtle than the kitchen. Carter placed the vase in the center of the table, then turned to help Sophia as she followed with a platter of sandwiches and a bowl of salad.

After a final trip to bring in plates, silverware and drinks, they settled across from each other. "Thanks for doing this," Carter said, snagging a sandwich while Sophia added salad to her plate. "I would have been happy to pick up food and bring it over."

"It's not a problem," Sophia responded. "I don't mind cooking, though you can't really call this cooking."

"I do," he replied. "It's homemade, so I think that counts."

They started chatting, a little haltingly at first. But soon they were talking like old friends, catching up on each other's lives. She told him about her apartment in El Paso, her friends in graduate school and what her studies were like. Carter listened, fascinated.

"Have you been camping in Big Bend?" he asked. "Depending on the weather, you can see some amazing views of the Milky Way. I imagine if you brought a telescope it would be even more incredible."

Sophia shook her head. "I always wanted to do that, but somehow never got around to it while I was here."

"I can take you sometime," he offered without thinking. But could he really? Most of the best stargazing spots were remote, accessible via trails or the river. He wasn't exactly cut out for backcountry hiking at the moment. Disappointment swelled in his chest at the reminder of his limitations.

But if Sophia noticed his change in mood, she didn't show it. "That would be nice," she said, smiling a little.

There was a slight hesitation in her voice that caught his attention. It was something he'd noticed throughout their conversation. She'd seemed happy to talk to him, but he couldn't shake the feeling she was holding something back.

"Do you mind if I ask you about the accident?" She sounded almost apologetic, as though she was afraid of offending him.

"Not at all," he replied. Normally, he didn't like to talk about it, preferring instead to focus on the here and now. But it felt good to talk to Sophia. For the first time in a long time, he talked about his feelings; how he'd thought he was dying, how in his darkest moments in the early days of his recovery he'd wished he had died. She listened to him without interruption, giving him the space to tell his story. But her face made it clear she was no passive listener—her expressions ranged from sympathetic to encouraging, and there were even times her eyes shone with tears on his behalf.

"So that's my sob story," he said, leaning back in his chair.

Sophia shook her head. "I'm so sorry you went through that," she said softly. "I can only imagine how difficult things were for you."

"It was hard," he admitted. "Still is, some days. But my sister moved out here to help me, and that's made a huge difference."

She nodded, staring at her lap. "I'm sorry I didn't contact you. Danny told me about your fall and kept me updated, but I should have reached out. I know I sent some cards, but that doesn't really count."

"It's okay," Carter said. He took a sip of water. "You were trying to start your new life in El Paso. Besides, there wasn't much you could do for me."

"I know, but…" She looked up, her eyes full of guilt. "After that night…" She trailed off.

He smiled. "We didn't make any promises to each other, remember?"

A flicker of emotion danced across her face. "I wanted to call. I wanted to talk to you. *Needed* to, in fact." There was a note of urgency in her tone that piqued his curiosity. It was clear she had something to say.

He held up his hands. "Well, I'm here now," he said, trying to sound light. "What's on your mind?"

She took a deep breath, clearly preparing herself for something. "Let's move to the living room." She stood before he had a chance to respond and began to gather up the detritus of their meal.

Carter got to his feet and helped carry dishes into the kitchen, his mind swirling as he wondered why Sophia seemed so uneasy. What could she have to tell him that would make her so nervous?

Oh, God, she's got a disease.

The thought made his stomach lurch, and he nearly dropped the plates he was carrying. But, no, he told himself. He knew he was fine, at least in that regard. He'd had so many medical tests over the last eighteen months, he felt certain he would know if he'd been infected with an STD after their encounter. Besides, they'd used protection.

She led him to the living room and he lowered himself to the sofa. Sophia sat next to him, her body tense.

Carter placed his hand on her knee. "Whatever it is," he told her gently, "it's going to be okay."

She nodded. "It's about that night," she began. "When we slept together."

Carter felt his heart crack. So she did have an infection. *Don't let it be HIV,* he pleaded with the universe. The thought of Sophia having to deal with the virus was too much to bear.

"Something else happened that night," she said.

He nodded, trying to keep his expression neutral. He didn't want her to know he'd already guessed what she was trying to say.

"Carter, I—"

A faint sound rang out from somewhere in the house. Sophia froze, a look of terror on her face. Then she cursed under her breath.

Carter frowned. "Is that a cat or something?" He didn't know she had a pet. Maybe she'd inherited it with the house?

"No," she said flatly. "I'll be right back."

She shot up from the couch and practically ran from the room, leaving him feeling a little discombobulated. This conversation was moving in a strange direction, and he wasn't sure what, exactly, was happening.

Sophia returned a moment later, an infant in her arms.

Carter stared at her, dumbfounded. "That's a baby,"

he said, trying to process the sight. "Who does it belong to?"

"Me," Sophia replied. Her expression was guarded as she walked into the room.

"Oh," he said reflexively. "When did you have a baby?"

"About nine months ago." She sat in the recliner next to the couch and began to rub the little one's back.

Carter nodded, still trying to accept this new turn of events. He'd thought Sophia was gearing up to tell him about a medical issue. But it seemed she'd been trying to tell him she'd become a mother.

Nine months…

Wait.

His brain kicked in and he started doing the math. He added up the time since she'd moved, the time since their encounter.

"But—"

It couldn't be.

They'd used a condom.

He met her gaze, saw the confirmation in her eyes. She nodded, lips pressed together.

"It's not possible," he whispered.

The baby squirmed in her arms. Sophia turned the infant around and Carter got his first glimpse of the little one's face.

His breath stalled in his chest as he saw his own eyes staring back at him.

"Carter," she said, her voice cracking. "I'd like you to meet your son."

* * *

Sophia held her breath. Her eyes locked on Carter's face as she watched him digest her words. This wasn't how she'd wanted things to go down. She'd wanted to tell him about Ben first, let him adjust to the idea of a baby. Then, after he'd had a chance to think about it for a little bit, she'd bring out Ben to meet him.

But their son had had other ideas.

Emotions played across Carter's face as he stared at Ben. Shock, disbelief, fear. She searched for a sign of pleasure, of a hint that maybe, just maybe, Carter was happy about the news that he was a father.

But all she saw was confusion.

"I don't understand," he said, sounding dazed. "We used a condom."

"I know," she replied. It was the same conversation she'd had with herself all those months ago. "My guess is that it was too old. I don't know how often Hank restocked the bathroom dispenser. That box might have been sitting on his shelf for years."

Carter shook his head. "This wasn't supposed to happen."

Pain lanced her heart, and she tightened her hold on her baby boy. She'd long ago stopped thinking of him as an accident. He was a surprise, yes. But not an accident.

Still, she couldn't deny that had been one of her first reactions, as well.

She bit her tongue, trying to give Carter the space to process his shock…since there was more to come.

He got to his feet. For a second, she thought he was

going to come closer so he could take a better look at Ben. But instead he started pacing, his gait a little halting without his cane. His face was so pale she thought he might pass out, and she shifted the baby on her lap, ready to help him if necessary.

"Why...?" He cleared his throat, then spoke again. "Why didn't you tell me about him? When you were pregnant, I mean."

"I didn't have your number," she said. "I called Danny to get it, and that's when I learned about your accident." Hitching in a breath, she ran her hand over Ben's hair. "From what he told me, you were on the verge of death. Then, once you'd stabilized, I knew it was going to take a lot of time for you to heal. I didn't think it would be fair to tell you that I was pregnant on top of everything else."

He stopped, turning to look at her. There was a wariness in his eyes as he glanced from her to the baby.

"Are you sure he's mine?" He regarded Ben as though he was a ticking bomb.

Anger washed over her in a sudden rush, darkening the edges of her vision. She glared at Carter, not bothering to hide her contempt. "Do you really think I'm the kind of person who would lie about my baby's paternity? That I would try to scam you about something as important as this?" She laughed bitterly. "Trust me—if that was the case, I would have picked a rich man instead."

Carter flinched as the barb hit home. He dropped his head. "I'm sorry. I didn't mean—"

"I know what you meant," she said evenly. "I haven't slept with anyone since you. Is that enough of an ego boost for you?"

He jerked up his head, eyes narrowing as he stared at her. "Why are you angry with me? I'm not the bad guy here!"

Sophia gaped at him. "You think *I* am?"

Carter threw up his hands. "You tell me! You're the one who kept the baby a secret all these months. When were you planning on telling me, exactly?" He took a step closer, his green eyes sparking with anger. "Be honest—if Will hadn't died and left you everything, and you weren't here right now, would you have told me about my son? Or would you still be in El Paso, with me none the wiser?"

"Of course I would have told you." But she heard the note of doubt in her voice. Yes, she would have told Carter. Eventually. The timing just always seemed to be off...

"Really?" His eyebrows shot up in an expression of disbelief. "Because I don't remember you mentioning a baby in any of your cards."

Sophia glanced away. "This isn't the kind of news you deliver in a letter."

"Which brings me back to my original point," he said tersely. "If Will hadn't died, when were you going to tell me?"

Ben started to squirm in her arms. Sophia set him on the ground and watched as he made a beeline for the coffee table. Carter watched him crawl, momentarily distracted by the sight.

She stood, skirting past Carter so she could be closer to the table in case Ben fell as he pulled up on the furniture. "Does it matter?" she asked, resignation creeping into her voice. "I'm here now."

"Yes, it matters!" he shouted.

She flinched, her muscles tensing. Carter had never seemed like a violent man before, but she didn't really know him, did she?

Regret danced across his face and he held up his hands in a gesture of surrender. "I'm sorry," he said quietly. He ran a hand through his hair, leaving the short strands standing on end.

Oblivious to the argument going on above him, Ben slapped his hand on the coffee table and bounced up and down.

Sophia stole a glance at Carter and found him watching the baby, his expression a mix of emotions.

"I'm sorry, too," she murmured softly. "I know I should have handled this better, but I didn't know what to do. I never meant to keep him a secret from you."

Carter's gaze stayed locked on Ben. His eyes were shiny with tears as he stared down at his son.

"His name is Ben," she told him. "Would you like to hold him?"

Carter straightened, as if a spell had been broken. "I have to go," he said abruptly.

Sophia bit her lip to keep from crying out. She'd known this was a possibility all along. She wasn't going to beg him to stay.

He turned on his heel and headed for the door. She stayed by Ben, gritting her teeth to keep the tears at bay.

The front door shut with a solid thunk, the sound seeming to echo in the house. Sophia sank onto the sofa, feeling hollowed-out.

A sudden pounding sent her heart into her throat.

She glanced at Ben, deciding he was fine for the moment. Then she walked to the front door, apprehension dogging each step.

Carter stood on the porch, fist raised to knock again. He dropped his hand and met her gaze.

"I'm not *leaving* leaving," he said. "This conversation is definitely not over. I just need some time."

Sophia nodded, a spark of relief flaring to life in her heart. "Okay," she whispered. That was fair. She had dropped a bomb on his life—it made sense he needed to process the news.

It was Carter's turn to nod. He stood there for a second, looking like he had more to say.

"All right," he said finally. "We'll talk again soon."

"You know where to find me," Sophia reminded him.

He turned and started down the path. After a few steps he stopped, then glanced back. "He's a cute kid," he said, jangling his keys in his hand.

Sophia felt a smile tug at her lips. "Very."

He started walking again. "Got your hair," he called back.

"And your eyes," she pointed out.

Carter paused at the door of his truck, considering her words. "Yes, he does."

It was a small acknowledgment, the type of off-hand comment people made every day. But the casual acceptance of his link to Ben hit her like a sledge-hammer.

Unaware of her reaction, Carter climbed into the driver's seat and started the ignition. He backed out into the street and offered her a little wave as he drove away.

Sophia stood in the doorway a moment, letting her emotions settle. That had gone as well as could be expected, she decided as she shut the door and returned to the living room. Carter hadn't been thrilled with the news that he was a father, but realistically, she knew it was a huge shock. The fact that he'd said he was coming back made her feel a lot better about the prospects of his future involvement in Ben's life.

But as she knelt down to play with the baby, worry still tugged at her heart. Carter would eventually adjust to the fact that he had a son, but how would he react when he discovered Ben was deaf?

Maybe I should have told him, she thought. How, though? Ben's very existence had sent Carter reeling. Would he have even heard her if she'd told him about their son's deafness, too?

Oh, by the way. There's one more thing you should know. That approach would probably have gone over about as well as a lead balloon.

No, better to do this in stages. Let him adjust to one piece of information before adding another. Maybe he'd be upset that she hadn't laid it all out at once. If so, that was just too bad. She was trying her best, navigating these tricky waters without any sort of guide.

She sighed, shaking her head. She'd thought she would feel relief once Carter knew about the baby. But her fears hadn't diminished. If anything, she was more scared than ever.

Telling Carter had been the right thing to do. Deep down, she knew that.

But his life wasn't the only one changing. Sophia felt a sense of helplessness, like things were now spinning out of her control.

Was that the price of honesty? Or a premonition of things to come?

Chapter 7

Carter moved on autopilot, navigating the streets of Alpine with no real awareness of where he was going.

In his mind, he replayed the scene over and over again. Sophia walking back into the living room, a baby in her arms.

I'd like you to meet your son.

Her words echoed in his head, drowning out the sounds of the engine, the blast of the air conditioner, the song on the radio.

Your son.

"It's not possible," he muttered.

He shook his head, trying to dislodge the memory. Maybe it was all a dream, the result of mixing his medication with a few beers at the show last night.

Except, his back ached. He never felt pain in his dreams.

Once more, his thoughts circled back to that moment when everything had changed.

She had a baby.

His baby.

It just didn't make sense. They'd done everything right—taken all the necessary precautions to make sure something like this didn't happen.

But…it had. He'd seen the kid with his own eyes.

The boy was practically his double, except for his hair. That had come from Sophia. But as for the rest… it was clear he was a Donaghey. Same chin, same eyes, same nose. No, there was no mistaking the resemblance.

So what now?

He pulled into a parking spot and cut the engine. He glanced at the sign on the building and snorted. Rickey's Garage. Hopefully Danny was still at work.

Carter climbed out of the truck, belatedly realizing he'd left his cane at Sophia's. He headed for the door, ignoring the Closed sign in the window. Danny often stayed later on Saturdays to put in some work on his pet project—restoring a 1949 Ford F-1 truck.

The front bay doors of the shop were closed, so as to discourage drop-ins. He glanced through the glass panes and saw one back bay door was open. Relief flooded him at the sight—Danny was here.

He walked slowly around the building, wondering what he was going to say. A surprise baby wasn't exactly the kind of thing you just blurted out. But it also wasn't a topic that came up in regular conversation.

Doesn't matter, he decided. No matter how he broke the news, Danny was going to be shocked. But after his initial reaction, Carter hoped his friend would have some good advice for him.

Classic rock blared from an old boom box on a workbench. He heard the clinking of tools as he entered the bay. The hood of the old truck was open, and Danny's voice drifted out from behind it as he sang along to the music.

"You should stick to the drums," Carter said loudly, hoping his voice carried above the din of the radio and the whir of the shop fan.

Danny poked his head around the hood. "Whatever, man. I sound fabulous."

"You sound like a drowning goat."

"Well, don't sugarcoat it for me." His pal picked up a grease-stained rag and began wiping his hands. "Did you come to my shop just to insult me, or is there something else you needed?"

"I was hoping we could talk."

Danny studied his face for a moment, his eyes kind. "Sure thing. Let's go into the office. The AC is on, and I've got some cold drinks in the fridge."

"Thanks, man."

He followed his friend into the main office, then back into a smaller room off the lobby. Danny gestured to the sofa, so Carter sat while his friend opened the fridge. "Water? Or we've got Coke. Also a couple of beers."

"Just water, thanks."

Danny tossed him a bottle before taking one for himself. Then he sat in a chair and stretched his legs out in front of him, turning his face up to the ceiling fan. "Ahhh," he said.

"It's a hot one today," Carter observed. As a park ranger, he'd built up a tolerance to the heat. But ever since his accident, he'd had a hard time handling the high temperatures. He'd spent so much time in air-conditioned hospital rooms, doctors' offices and therapy gyms that he'd gone soft.

"Mmm-hmm," Danny agreed. "So what's going on? I figured you'd still be having lunch with Sophia." He grinned slyly. "After last night, it looked like you guys had some catching up to do."

Boy, did they. "I just left there, actually." He turned the bottle in his hands, trying to organize his thoughts. "She had a surprise for me."

Danny huffed out a laugh. "I bet she did. But if it's all the same to you, I don't need details. The last thing I need is to picture you naked."

"That wasn't the surprise," Carter said, ignoring the jab. "She, uh…she had a baby."

Danny's eyes widened. "Really? I had no idea. When did that happen?"

"About nine months ago."

His friend leaned back in his chair, calculating. "Wow. So she met someone right away after moving to El Paso."

"Not exactly," Carter said. He started to peel the label off the water bottle, unable to meet Danny's eyes.

The other man swore softly. "It's yours, isn't it?"

Carter nodded. "It's mine." It felt strange to say the words out loud. To acknowledge that he was the father of Sophia's baby. A weight landed on his shoulders, as though telling Danny about his son had somehow made things even more real.

"Whoa." Danny shook his head, sounding as shocked as Carter had felt. *Still* felt, if he was being honest.

"I always thought you two had something going on," he continued. "James told me I was just imagining things, but—" he tapped his temple with his forefinger "—I'm smarter than I look."

Carter had to smile. "I've never doubted you. But we weren't together, not really. We had a one-night stand her last night at the bar. She moved the next day, and I didn't think I'd see her again."

"Why didn't you guys ever hook up before? There was always chemistry between you two. Anyone could see it."

Carter shrugged. "I guess I was afraid. She never seemed like the kind for a fling, and since we all knew her stay in Alpine wasn't long-term, I didn't want to get involved and risk falling for her."

His friend tilted his head to the side. "Fair enough. But a one-night stand is pretty much the definition of a fling."

"True. I think at that point, we just figured it was our last opportunity to be together." He hadn't spoken to Sophia about that night specifically, but the knowledge that she'd no longer be in Alpine had weakened his resolve to stay away from her. If their connection hadn't extended to the bedroom, they would have parted ways without having to deal with any awkward future encounters. The circumstances had been perfect for a test of their sexual compatibility—a test that they'd passed with flying colors.

And then some.

"So..." Danny trailed off, and Carter got the sense his friend was trying to figure out how to phrase his next thought. "Did you guys not use protection?"

"That's the thing," Carter replied. "We did."

"Wow. Super sperm!"

Carter snorted. "Hardly."

"I take it you just now found out about the baby?"

Carter nodded. "He woke up while we were talking. She brought him out of the bedroom and introduced him to me."

"Him?"

"Yeah. His name is Ben."

Danny shook his head. "What a way to learn you're a dad."

"Tell me about it. I just wish she'd said something before now."

The other man's expression changed, a growing realization replacing his surprise. "So that's why she called," he said softly.

"What?" Carter's tone sharpened. What was he talking about?

"The day after your accident, Sophia called me. She wanted to know how to get in touch with you. I assumed she'd heard about your fall—it was on the news at the time. But she seemed surprised when I told her about it." He was quiet a moment, clearly trying to recall the conversation. "She gave me her number and asked me to keep her updated on your condition. Once you'd started to recover, I gave her your address. She said she wanted to send you cards."

"She did," Carter confirmed.

"You fell about a month after she left," Danny said. "She must have just learned she was pregnant."

"But she never mentioned it to you? Never hinted that something was going on?"

Danny shook his head. "Nope. Do you really think I'd have kept something like that from you if I knew?" He sounded hurt.

"No, I didn't mean to suggest that." Carter ran a hand through his hair. "I'm just trying to wrap my brain around the fact that she had a kid. There's this whole new person in the world, and I'm responsible for it."

Danny didn't respond. Silence hung in the air, heavy and thick. Finally, his friend spoke again. "Man." He shook his head. "What are you going to do?"

"I don't know," Carter said honestly. "I mean, I'm going to support the baby. I've been thinking about maybe transitioning into teaching, since realistically I don't think I can go back to being a ranger. And I do want to be part of his life." He blew out a breath. "But I'm not sure how that will work, with her living in El Paso and me living here. Plus, right now, I'm still a little angry with her. It's going to take some time for me to work through that."

"You're mad 'cause she kept the pregnancy a secret?"

Carter nodded. "Hell yes! Wouldn't you be, in my position?"

Danny lifted one shoulder. "Yes and no. I mean, try to see it from her perspective. She found out she's pregnant, so she tried to call you, only to learn you'd been in a terrible accident and might die. It wasn't exactly the best time to let you know the condom broke."

"I understand why she didn't tell me right away," Carter replied. "But the baby is nine months old. That's a long time to keep his existence a secret. And the worst part is that if she hadn't inherited that house from Will, I don't know when she would have told me. When he's five? Sixteen? When, exactly, would it have been the right time to let me know I have a son?" Anger seeped into his voice as his temper rose.

Danny held up his hands. "I'm not trying to make excuses for her," he said. "But something like this... The longer you keep a secret, the bigger it gets. Maybe she was scared because so much time had passed?"

"Maybe," Carter acknowledged. He knew it hadn't been easy for Sophia to talk to him. And he knew she hadn't wanted to just spring the baby on him—she'd meant to tell him first, before making the introductions.

But he was scared, too, dammit. She'd had an entire pregnancy to prepare for motherhood. Then she'd had nine months of taking care of the baby, learning his every expression, his cries, the way he moved.

He'd been presented with a stranger. A cute stranger, but a stranger nonetheless.

"I know you're upset," Danny said. "And you have every right to be. But don't let your anger toward Sophia keep you from getting to know your son. If you really want to be part of his life, you have to start now. Don't lose any more time with him."

And there it was. The sage advice Carter had hoped Danny would provide.

"You're right." He sighed, knowing it was the truth. He could either hold on to his anger, or he could get to know Ben. It wasn't possible to do both.

"I'm here for you," Danny said. "James, too. Anything you need, just say the word."

Carter smiled, touched by the offer of support. "I know it," he said. "And thanks."

"Of course." His friend brushed aside his gratitude. "That's what friends do. How much longer will Sophia be in town?"

"I'm not sure," Carter replied. It was a question he'd meant to ask, but Ben's appearance had thrown his thoughts into such chaos he could barely remember how to spell his own name. "I know she's trying to go through the house and get it ready to sell."

"Maybe you could help. It'd be good for you to all spend time together."

Carter nodded. "Yeah. If she'll let me."

"I think she will," Danny said. "I think she wants you to be part of the baby's life. If she didn't, she wouldn't have told you about him at all."

Carter hadn't even considered that possibility. The

idea sent a little shock down his spine. His pal was right—she had been under no obligation to see him, to tell him about Ben. She could have snuck into town and lain low until the house was sold, and he would have never known otherwise. "I suppose that's true."

He got to his feet, missing his cane as he moved, then tossed his empty water bottle into the trash. Danny followed suit, then clapped him on the shoulder.

"You've got a family of your own. Can you believe it?"

Carter shook his head. No, not yet.

But it was starting to sink in.

"Mr. Randolph will see you now."

Jake smiled at the secretary and followed her through the door into the lawyer's office. The formality of it all was ridiculous—the lobby was barely larger than a broom closet, and as he glanced around, he saw the office wasn't much bigger. Not to mention, the place had been empty when he'd walked in, so it wasn't like there was a need for crowd control.

No, he thought to himself as the secretary announced his arrival. It seemed that Mr. Randolph was one of those men who thought he was important, so rather than accepting the reality that he was practicing law in this dusty little Texas town, he acted like he was master of the universe.

The man in question stood and offered his hand. "Mr. Porter, it's nice to meet you."

"Likewise." Jake could be nice when the occasion called for it.

Randolph settled into his seat, gesturing for Jake to take one of the chairs in front of his desk. "How can I help you today?"

"I believe you assisted my grandfather with his will."

"That's possible," the older man replied. "Estate planning is one of my specialties."

It was more than possible; Jake was already certain Randolph had been his grandfather's attorney. He'd gone through the list of lawyers in Alpine, and everyone else had confirmed his grandpa had not been a client.

"His name was Will Porter—William Porter," Jake amended. "He died about six months ago."

Something flickered in Randolph's eyes—a gleam of calculation, perhaps? "Yes, Mr. Porter was one of my clients."

Jake nodded. "I'm here today because I believe there's been a mistake."

"Oh?" Randolph was guarded now. When he spoke again, there was a note of wariness in his voice. "What makes you think that?"

Time to lay on the charm. Jake smiled and leaned forward, adopting a just-between-us expression. "Well, you see, my grandfather told me that I was due to inherit his home and possessions after he died. We spoke about it several times." The lie tripped off his tongue easily, a result of years of bluffing his way out of a bad hand. "Grandpa wanted me to raise my own family there."

"I see," Randolph said, though his tone made it clear he didn't.

"You can imagine my surprise when I went to the house and found a woman already living there."

"Mmm-hmm" was the noncommittal reply.

Jake frowned slightly, unable to get a read on Randolph. The attorney was keeping things very close to the vest; he was probably an excellent card player.

But it didn't matter. Jake had gone up against the best and lived to tell the tale. This would be no different.

He decided to go on the offensive. "I'd like to know what that woman is doing in my home. It's clear there's been some kind of misunderstanding, and I want it cleared up as soon as possible."

Randolph narrowed his eyes slightly, considering. "Mr. Porter, I'm very sorry for your loss. I'm sure the death of your grandfather came as quite a shock, as did the discovery that you were not a beneficiary of his estate."

Jake nodded, adopting an earnest expression. But inside, his frustration mounted. This guy wasn't going to help him; he could tell that much already. Still, he might be able to learn something useful.

"Now, I believe we posted a death announcement, as is required. Let me check…" He made a show of looking at his computer, clicking here and there to bring up a file. "Ah, yes." Randolph swiveled the monitor around so Jake could see the screen. It was a text document, stating that William Porter of Alpine, Texas, had died and that any person who had business with or claims against his estate was to come forward and be heard.

"As you can see," Randolph continued, "the date for claims against the estate has passed. Your grandfather's will has been executed by the state, and there's nothing to be done about it now."

Anger and panic bubbled in Jake's chest. There had to be another option, another way for him to get his money. "You mean to tell me my grandfather didn't leave me anything?" He heard the edge in his voice but no longer cared about presenting a calm image to the lawyer.

Randolph shook his head somberly. "No."

"But I saw his will!" It was the truth—the old man had let him read it years ago, back when he'd shown Jake the location of the fire safe, where he kept his important documents.

"Just in case you ever need to know where it is," his grandfather had said.

"You may have seen an earlier version of the document," Randolph replied. "But the most recent version that my office prepared for your grandfather supersedes any older documents."

"That's not right!" Jake was rapidly losing his grip on his temper. "When did he make the changes?"

The attorney glanced at the computer screen, did some more clicking with the mouse. "Approximately three months before he died."

Jake's mind whirled. Why had his grandfather cut

him out of the will? And why had he left everything to that woman?

She really was a gold digger, he realized. It was the only explanation.

But how could he undermine her claim to his inheritance? *Think, think, think...*

"I don't believe my grandfather was of sound mind when he revised his will," Jake declared. That sounded official, didn't it?

Randolph narrowed his eyes and leaned back in his chair. "What is the basis for your claim?"

"He left everything to this woman, a stranger. I believe she took advantage of an old man, had him change his will to leave her everything."

"Perhaps," Randolph said. "But your suspicion is not enough evidence to prove Mr. Porter was incapacitated when he revised the document."

"What do I need to do to prove it?" How hard could it be? His grandfather had been old, and dementia ran in the family. Surely he could make a solid case that Will hadn't really meant to cut him out of the will.

"Medical evidence, for starters."

"Fine. I'll talk to his doctors," Jake said.

"There's more to it—"

"What about the original will?"

Randolph nodded. "That would be necessary, as well. But—"

"Done." Jake didn't have the document, but he knew exactly where it was inside the house. It wouldn't take long to find it.

"Mr. Porter, you must understand. Even if you have

an older version of the will and speak to your grand-father's doctors, there is no guarantee the situation will change. William was very clear about his wishes—"

"I don't care," Jake interrupted. He shoved to his feet and leaned over the desk, forcing Randolph to scoot back in his chair. "His money, his house, his things—it's all mine. I don't know who that bitch is or how she conned me out of my inheritance. But I'm not going to just roll over and let her get away with it. I'll get your proof, and then we'll see who has the last laugh."

Randolph opened his mouth to respond, but Jake spun on his heel and walked out of the room before the other man could speak. He was done listening to the lies, the prevarications, the smug pronouncements of what he could or could not do. He was tired of being passive.

It was time to act.

Chapter 8

The doorbell rang just as Sophia wrestled Ben to the floor for a diaper change.

"Leah, can you get that, please?"

"No problem!" the younger girl called out.

Leah had arrived two hours ago to help her with Project Organization, the name she'd given to the seemingly endless task of sorting through the contents of Will's house. They were still working in the living room, boxing up rows and rows of books. Sophia still didn't know what she was going to do with them. It seemed wrong to throw away books, but a representative from the library had already been by and taken all the volumes they wanted for their collection. She'd been disappointed at the small stack the woman had left with, knowing it had barely made a dent in Will's collection.

Ben writhed on the floor, trying to escape so he could resume his explorations of the room. Sophia worked fast, trying to put the clean diaper on his bottom before he could either pee again or make a getaway.

"Uh, Soph? Can you come here?"

"Just a minute," she called out, holding her son down. A flicker of worry crossed her mind. What if that man from earlier had come back? Maybe she should have ignored the doorbell instead of sending her younger cousin to deal with the visitor.

She secured the final tab of the diaper and released Ben. He immediately rolled over and crawled for the nearest box. He thought it was great fun to stand and pull the books out of the box, dropping them to the floor one by one.

Sophia wrapped up his old diaper and headed for the door. "What's going on?"

The question died in her throat when she saw Carter standing on the welcome mat, a pizza box in hand.

"Hi," he said carefully. He seemed uncertain, as though he didn't know how she would respond to his appearance.

"Hi," Sophia echoed. She'd deliberately spent the afternoon working so that she didn't have to think about their lunch or agonize over his earlier reactions. It had been difficult—her heart had wanted nothing more than to dive into the nearest gallon of ice cream and eat her feelings away. But she'd known it wouldn't solve anything. So she'd put on a brave face and tried to move forward, struggling to make peace with the fact that she couldn't control Carter or his actions.

Part of her was elated to see him. He'd said he was coming back, and now here he was, making good on his word. It was a hopeful sign. Maybe the first of many to come?

He lifted the box. "Peace offering?"

She smiled. "Depends," she replied. "What kind?"

Worry crossed his face. Then he met her eyes and realized she was joking. "Sausage and mushroom," he said.

"That'll do." Sophia reached for the box. "Come on in."

She moved back so he could walk inside. As she turned, she saw Leah. The young woman glanced from her to Carter and back again. "I think I'll head out," she said.

"You don't have to go," Sophia protested.

Carter spoke at the same time. "The pizza is big enough for everyone."

Sophia glanced at him, wondering if he wanted Leah to stay so he wouldn't have to be alone with her. But she dismissed the thought with her next breath. He hadn't known Leah was here before he stopped by. If he truly didn't want to see her one-on-one, he would have asked her to meet somewhere public.

"No, it's okay," Leah said, grabbing her bag from the table in the entry hall. "I told Mom I'd pick up some milk on the way home. I'd better get going."

She reached for the diaper Sophia still held. "I'll take that. You've got your hands full."

"Thanks for your help today."

"Sure thing." Leah leaned forward to embrace her. "You okay?" she whispered.

"Yeah," Sophia whispered back.

"Is that him?"

"Yep."

"Good luck."

Sophia released her cousin. "See you tomorrow?" she asked.

Leah nodded. "You bet." She gave a little wave to Carter, who was standing nearby, pretending not to have heard their whispering. "See you."

He smiled. "Goodbye."

Sophia closed the door behind Leah, then turned to face Carter. "That was my cousin. She's been helping me with the house and with Ben."

"She seems nice."

"She's a sweet kid. Going to graduate high school next spring." She put the pizza on the dining-room table and headed for the living room. "Let me check on him. Then we can eat."

"I, uh…" Carter cleared his throat, then asked, "Can I help?"

Surprise washed over her, though she tried not to let it show. "Sure," she said. "He's in the living room." She led the way down the hall, careful not to walk too fast. "You left your cane here earlier."

"I know," he replied. "I realized it when I was halfway to home."

"Is that why you're here? To get it back?" She held her breath, awaiting his reply. The fact that he'd returned made her feel better, but she didn't want to assume he'd come because he wanted to be Ben's dad. It was possible he was here to tell her he wanted nothing to do with them.

"Partly," Carter said. If he sensed her tension, he didn't show it. "But mainly I was hoping we could finish talking."

Sophia nodded as they stepped into the room. "I'd like that."

Ben spied her and let out a squeal. He dropped the book he was holding and headed her way. She bent down and picked him up, pressing a kiss to his chubby cheek.

Ben tolerated her affections, his eyes glued to Carter as he took stock of their visitor. Carter smiled at the boy. "Hey there," he said gently. "How are you today?" He reached up with one hand and tickled Ben's foot.

The baby giggled, then turned and buried his face in Sophia's neck. "He's a little shy," she explained.

"Nothing wrong with that," Carter said, his gaze still on the baby.

"Let's head for the kitchen," she suggested. "I need to wash my hands and I'll grab some plates."

"Do you think he'll let me hold him?"

The question made her stomach flip-flop. "We can try," she said. Hopefully Ben would cooperate, but there was no guarantee.

Sophia walked over to the sink, Carter trailing

close behind. Ben's curiosity had apparently gotten the better of his fear, as he was now openly watching Carter. Without giving him a chance to protest, Sophia quickly passed Ben over to his father.

Carter shifted Ben so that they were facing each other. "Whoa," he said. "You're heavier than you look."

Sophia instinctively reached for the baby, but Carter waved her off. "I've got him," he reassured her. "We're okay, aren't we, little man?"

She watched them for a moment, man and baby, her heart swelling as she saw the look of tenderness on Carter's face, the flash of awe in his eyes as he held his son for the first time. He blinked hard, and she realized he was on the verge of tears.

For his part, Ben studied his father with a serious expression on his little face. Carter took his free hand and tickled the baby's foot again, sticking his tongue out at the same time. Ben giggled, so Carter did it once more.

The baby's laughter washed over Sophia, and for a moment, she felt at peace. This, right here, the three of them together and happy—it was what she'd been dreaming of for so long. She knew the moment wouldn't last forever, but she closed her eyes, determined to absorb everything about this little slice of perfection so she could relive it later.

"You okay?"

Carter's question pulled her out of her reverie. She opened her eyes, smiled at the two of them. "Yeah," she said quietly. "Just taking it all in."

His green eyes brimmed with emotion. "I know what you mean."

It was going to be all right, she realized. They still had a lot to discuss, and there were things she hadn't told him yet. But she felt their connection grow stronger as the moment stretched on.

He'd come back. It was enough for now.

Something inside her eased, a knot of tension and stress and fear she'd been carrying for far too long. There was a chance Carter could still walk away, especially after finding out that Ben was deaf. But in this moment, they were a family.

Ben shifted in Carter's arms, reaching for the sunglasses his dad had pushed up to rest on the top of his head. Carter beat him to it, taking the glasses and holding them for Ben's inspection. "Wanna try them on?"

He slipped them over Ben's face, holding them in place so they didn't slide off. Ben went still, taking in the world from this new perspective. One chubby hand lifted to touch the frames, his fingerprints smearing across the lens. He grinned, his two bottom teeth flashing in the kitchen light.

Sophia laughed at the adorable sight. Carter smiled. "They look better on you than me," he told the baby.

He retrieved the glasses before Ben could do any damage. Sophia turned to the sink and washed her hands, enjoying the sound of Carter talking to Ben. She moved a few steps away to retrieve plates from the cabinet.

"What's that? You want your mom?" he asked.

Then he said, "I didn't know you're teaching him baby sign language. That's cool."

Sophia froze, her hand on the knob of the cabinet. "How do you know sign language?" she asked, dodging the issue.

"My sister," Carter said.

She relaxed a bit. "Oh, she has kids?" It would be nice for Ben to have some cousins.

"No," Carter replied. "She's Deaf."

Ice shot through Sophia's body. Her fingers went numb, and the plates slipped through her grip to land on the counter with a clatter.

She felt Carter at her elbow. "Hey, you okay? Did you cut yourself?"

Sophia shook her head, angling her body so she kept her back to Carter. She had to get her emotions under control first. "No, I'm good. I don't think anything broke. I—I think my hands were still a little wet, that's all."

"It happens."

She carefully gathered the plates again. "Tell me more about your sister," she said, trying to keep her voice neutral. "I remember you said earlier she was staying with you."

"Mmm-hmm," Carter replied. She stole a glance over her shoulder and saw him focused on Ben. "Her name is Margot. She's three years younger than me."

"And you said she's Deaf?"

"Yeah."

Sophia swallowed hard, gathering her courage to ask the next question. "Was she...?" She cleared her throat, tried again. "Was Margot born deaf? Or did something happen?"

"No, she was born that way," Carter said. "Why all the curiosity about my sister?"

And here it was. The moment of truth. "Carter, there's something else you need to know about Ben." She turned around and met his eyes.

Carter frowned, tightening his hold on the baby in an unconscious gesture of protection. "What's going on?" he asked. "You sound upset."

"I should have told you this earlier—" she began.

"Well, just tell me now," Carter interrupted. There was an edge in his voice, a note of worry that hadn't been there before.

She closed her eyes, pressing her lips together as she tried to dredge up the words. Why couldn't they have had a little more time? Just a few more minutes together as a family before plunging into the challenges of reality again?

"Sophia." Carter's tone was soft, almost pleading. "Just say it. Please."

She opened her eyes, wanting to see his face when she broke the news. Then she spoke the words that would change…everything.

"Ben is deaf."

For the second time that day, Carter found himself staring at Sophia, unable to speak.

Deaf?

He's deaf?

He looked down at the baby in his arms, trying to

reconcile this news with the squirming boy he held to his chest. Ben grunted, pushing his hand down forcefully.

"Oh," Carter said numbly, finally catching on. The baby was trying to make the sign for *down*.

He knelt carefully, ignoring the aching in his hips, and placed Ben on the floor. Apparently deciding the adults weren't entertaining enough, Ben started to crawl toward the other room.

Carter stood, his hand on the counter for support. When he looked at Sophia again, he saw her eyes were bright with tears.

"I'm sorry," she whispered. "I wanted to tell you earlier. I didn't mean to keep another secret from you."

"It's okay," he replied automatically. He shook his head, the cobwebs clearing from his mind. "I know why you waited."

And he did. Earlier, when he'd first learned about Ben's existence, he hadn't exactly given her a chance to share this information. Even if she had told him, he'd been so blown away by the shock of finding out he was a father he probably wouldn't have heard her.

A muffled thump came from the other room. "We should probably—" He gestured to the dining area.

Sophia wiped her nose with the back of her hand. "Yeah," she said, voice thick with emotion. "No telling what he's getting into out there."

She took a few steps toward him, then headed out of the kitchen. Carter reached up and grabbed her arm before she could move past. "Hey," he said softly.

He waited for her to meet his eyes. Emotions swirled in her gaze: apprehension, fear...and a glint of sheer determination. *She's a warrior*, he realized with a growing sense of awe. For the first time since learning about Ben, he caught a glimpse of how hard things had been for her. Being pregnant alone. Having a baby by herself, no one by her side to cheer her on during the delivery. The sleepless nights, the countless feedings and diaper changes. The terror she must have felt, knowing something was wrong with her baby.

She'd done it all alone, with no one to help her. And she'd managed to work on her studies, as well.

She was a damn superhero.

Carter was humbled by her strength. He'd thought his own situation had been tough. How many hours had he spent feeling sorry for himself, thinking things couldn't get worse? All the while, Sophia had been working night and day to care for a baby. A baby she hadn't planned on, either.

He suddenly felt very small, standing next to her. How much grief had he caused her today? How much stress and worry had he added to her already full plate? He'd handled things badly earlier. But he was here now, and he was determined to step up and do his job as a father and as a man.

"It's okay," he told her. "Really."

She held his gaze for a moment, as though trying to judge his sincerity. He didn't look away, wanting her to know he meant what he'd said. For better or for worse, Ben was his son. Carter wasn't going to walk away from him now, just because the baby was deaf.

Some of the fear left her face as his words sank in. He felt the tension leave her muscles, and he realized with a shock that she'd braced herself for a totally different reaction.

My God, he thought, trying to see things through her eyes. Of course she'd been scared. She'd had no way of knowing what he'd say or do after finding out Ben wasn't perfect. She hadn't known about Margot, hadn't known about Carter's experiences with Deaf culture or sign language. For the second time that day, she'd exposed herself to him, knowing he could very well leave without looking back.

He wanted to gather her close, wrap his arms around her and press her to his chest. Tell her she didn't have to worry, that she didn't have to do this on her own anymore. He was here. Ben was his, and he intended to be a father to his son. He wanted to alleviate some of her worries, to share her burdens and ease the way so she didn't break under the weight of all those responsibilities she'd shouldered without complaint.

How could he tell her? What could he say to convince her to trust him, to let him help?

Carter opened his mouth, but another thump interrupted the moment. Sophia's eyes widened. "Oh, boy," she muttered, pulling away from him.

He followed her into the dining room just in time to see her extricate Ben from the frame of his high chair. "He was trying to climb into his seat," she said, holding him in one arm and using the other hand to try to remove the tray from the chair.

Carter stepped forward and slid the tray free. She

plopped Ben into the seat and quickly buckled him in. Then she turned and took the tray from Carter, sliding it into place.

"Guess he's hungry," Carter said, smiling at the baby's determination.

Ben pointed to the pizza box on the table, then brought his hand to his mouth. "You wanna eat, buddy?" Carter asked, recognizing the sign. He sat next to the baby and pulled the box closer. Then he glanced up at Sophia. "Can he have regular food? Or does he need something different?"

"He can have table food," she replied. "I usually pick the toppings off and give them to him. Small bites only, though. I'm going to grab some orange slices and an avocado for him, as well. Are you okay here?"

Carter nodded, already pulling mushrooms and pieces of sausage out of the cheese. He made sure they were cool, then placed them on Ben's tray. The boy grabbed the food with both hands, stuffing as much as he could into his mouth.

"Slow down, buddy," Carter said, his heart starting to pound. Sophia had just told him the baby only needed small bites. If he choked now, she'd never forgive him. "Uh, he's shoving a lot in there at once," he called out.

"He does that," she replied. She returned a moment later with a plate bearing mandarin oranges and sliced avocado. "I asked the pediatrician about it, since I was worried he would choke. She said as long as the individual bites are small, he should be okay."

Carter relaxed a bit, because of her words and her return to the room. His knowledge of babies could fit in a teaspoon, with room to spare. He was going to need a lot of guidance as he got to know Ben and figured out what the little one needed. Hopefully Sophia would be willing to help him.

She settled into the chair next to Ben, keeping a close eye on the baby as he ate. As the minutes ticked by, he realized he enjoyed watching his son eat. Ben fed himself with gusto, reaching for food and bringing it to his mouth with more enthusiasm than skill. His expressions were mercurial; a smile morphing into a frown in the blink of an eye when he tasted something he didn't like. Carter had to laugh when a piece of mushroom made it into Ben's mouth and was summarily rejected, the baby screwing up his face in disgust as he ejected the offending bit with his tongue.

"Is he always so expressive when he eats?"

"Oh, yeah," Sophia said. "He makes no secret of his likes and dislikes."

"Can you tell me about his diagnosis?" It was a serious topic, but he figured now was the best time to talk. Ben was occupied, which meant he couldn't get into anything at the moment. "How did you figure out he's deaf?"

"He failed the hearing test in the hospital," Sophia answered. She went on to describe the doctors' visits, the tests, the waiting. Sympathy and guilt swirled in his chest as he listened. She never once talked about herself, or how hard it had been for her, but he could read between the lines.

"I can only imagine how you must have felt," he said quietly. "I'm sorry I wasn't there to help."

She gave him a half smile. "You had your own problems," she reminded him. "And besides, you didn't even know. After I got the diagnosis, I was even more determined to wait to tell you. I figured it would be hard enough to learn you had a son. But finding out he was deaf, too?" She shook her head. "I worried it would derail your recovery."

There was some truth to her words. Nine months ago, his rehab had still been intense. He'd just had another surgery, and all his focus had been on recovery. If he'd learned about Ben at that time, he wouldn't have been able to handle everything. It pained him to even think about it, but he likely would have been no help at all. In fact, he probably would have pushed them away to focus on himself, forever poisoning his relationship with them and wrecking any chance of getting to know his son.

Still, he hated the circumstances that had kept them apart. "Did you have any support? Any family help?"

Sophia shook her head. "My parents are…gone," she said. "My mom died five years ago. My dad split when I was two."

"I didn't know that," he murmured. No wonder she was so strong—with a childhood like that, she'd had to be.

Sophia shrugged. "My aunts helped as much as they could. They sent diapers, clothes, a little money.

But my family isn't rich, and any extra money they have goes to keep my grandfather in the care facility."

"How's he doing?" Carter knew she'd worked at the bar while living with her grandfather, helping to take care of him while he was in the early stages of dementia. He remembered the day she'd helped move the older man into the care facility. He'd played a show that night, and Sophia had been in a strange mood, both sad and somehow lighter at the same time.

"Not so great," Sophia replied. "They're very sweet to him, but he's deteriorating. He doesn't recognize my aunts anymore. About the only things he does seem to remember are a few songs from his childhood."

"Music is funny that way," Carter said. "It gets inside of you and becomes a part of your soul."

He glanced at Ben, who was grinning widely behind a smear of tomato sauce and mashed avocado. A wave of sadness washed over Carter, taking his breath away. His son, this bright, happy boy, would never know the joy of a beautiful melody. He'd never hear the Beatles singing about love, never experience the power of a Beethoven symphony. Never feel the communion of a concert, and that strange, ephemeral connection forged with a crowd of strangers as everyone sang along with the band onstage.

He looked down, blinking hard. Music was such an important part of Carter's life. It was something he'd always thought he would share with his own children. But now...

Sophia put her hand on his. He jumped at the unexpected contact and looked up to find her watching him, understanding in her beautiful brown eyes.

"I know," she said, squeezing gently. "But the doctors say he'll still be able to enjoy music, just in a different way."

Carter sniffed, nodding. "They're right. Margot can feel the vibrations from a speaker, especially if the bass is really strong. There's even a deaf DJ she follows online. It's just…not the same."

"Maybe it's better?" Sophia suggested. She lifted one shoulder in an elegant shrug. "I've been thinking a lot about it, ever since I found out Ben couldn't hear. He won't be able to experience music the same way we do, but maybe he'll see differently, or taste things better, or smell things more intensely than we do. Maybe that will make up for his ears not working like they're supposed to."

"That's possible." He'd read about other senses becoming more highly attuned when one was gone. It was definitely a question for Margot, though how would she know? If you'd always smelled or tasted or seen a certain way, how could you compare it to anyone else?

"Anyway, he might be a candidate for a cochlear implant," Sophia continued. "So it's possible he'll eventually have some hearing."

Carter's thoughts snapped back into line at her words. "What?"

"A cochlear implant," she repeated.

"I heard what you said," he replied. "Are you seriously considering doing that to him?"

She frowned. "Well, I'm not crazy about the idea of him having surgery, but it's the only way to give him some degree of hearing."

"I don't think he needs it," Carter said. He knew from his sister that cochlear implants were a controversial issue in the Deaf community. Some people embraced the technology, while others disdained it, feeling it infringed on Deaf culture.

Sophia's eyes widened as she stared at him. "How can you say that? Don't you want him to have some semblance of hearing?"

Carter glanced away, struggling to articulate his thoughts. "He's not broken," he began. "I get that you want him to hear, because that's what you know. But from what I've read, the implants can be difficult. For people who aren't used to sound, it can be overwhelming. And when there's a lot of background noise, they're practically useless."

"Those are very specific situations," Sophia countered. "I doubt he'll have that much trouble."

"No?" Carter asked. He leaned forward in his seat. "What about when he's at school, changing classes? Or in the cafeteria? You think he'll be able to hear his friends over the din of everyone else's conversations? Forget about restaurants, malls, anything with crowds. He won't be able to hear tones very well, so a lot of social nuance will be a mystery. Why put him through that? So he can learn to interpret sounds in a narrow set of circumstances?"

Sophia's face reddened. "I don't think it's as bad as you say. The doctors—"

"The doctors see it as a cure for deafness, when it's not," Carter interrupted. "They don't know—"

"I want to be able to talk to my son!" Her voice rang out over his objections. "I want my baby to hear my voice."

Carter closed his mouth, absorbing her words. Sophia sank back into her chair, as though her outburst had drained her of energy. "I just want him to know what I sound like," she said dully.

His heart cracked at the sight of her, looking so dejected and hopeless. "I understand." And he did. As a hearing person, he took the sense for granted. Growing up with Margot had made him aware of the challenges Deaf people faced in a world built for sound. He knew it must have broken his parents' hearts to realize their daughter would never experience the love in their voices. But there were other ways of communicating. Other ways of showing affection, teasing someone, teaching them.

"Sophia," he said gently. He took a chance and reached for her hand. She didn't pull away, didn't reject his touch. "He knows you love him. You could take away all his senses, and he would still know you love him. He doesn't need his ears for that."

Tears tracked down her face as she met his eyes. "I just want him to have everything. Is that so wrong? Wanting to give him every advantage I can?"

"No, of course not," Carter replied. "I want what's best for him, too. I just don't know if that includes a cochlear implant." Inspiration struck like a bolt of lightning. "I think it would help if you talked to my sister."

Seeing Margot would help Sophia realize Ben could lead a full, joyful life without the use of implants. Margot could answer her questions, tell her about her experiences growing up Deaf. It would probably put Sophia's mind at ease to see how well Margot was doing, to know Ben could have that, too.

Sophia straightened, anxiety flitting across her face. "My sign language is terrible," she said. "I'm learning, but it's hard and it's taking me a while. I wouldn't want her to think I'm being rude."

"She won't," Carter assured her. "Margot doesn't offend easily."

"What did she say when she found out about Ben?" Sophia seemed almost shy, and Carter realized she must be worried that his sister thought badly of her for keeping the baby a secret for so long.

"We, ah...we haven't discussed it yet." Margot had texted him earlier in the day, letting him know her lunch with Mike was turning into a movie and dinner, as well. He hadn't seen her since dropping her off at the café earlier, so she was still unaware of her new status as aunt.

God, so much had changed in one day! He'd woken up this morning, excited about the possibility of rekindling the spark with Sophia. In a matter of hours, he'd learned he was a father and, moreover, that his son was deaf. It was a lot to take in, and in many ways, he was still reeling from the news.

Ben started pounding on the tray of his high chair, alternately signing *Mommy* and *down*.

"I think he's finished," Carter said. He turned to the little one and signed, *All done?*

Ben's eyes lit up and he started moving his hands, clearly attempting to communicate.

Carter nodded, repeating the sign. "Okay, all done," he said for Sophia's benefit. He helped her remove the tray and the restraints. "I'll get this," he said, gesturing to the remains of their dinner. "You get him."

"Thanks." She carried him into the living room while Carter cleared the table and put away the leftovers.

He walked to the living room and slowly lowered himself to the floor so he could be by Ben. It was going to be hard to get up later, but it was worth it to play with the boy. He and Sophia chatted while they played with the baby, the conversation growing smoother as time passed. Carter signed everything to Ben, knowing it was the best way for him to learn.

Sophia watched them, a smile playing on her lips. "How long did it take you to become fluent?"

"Not that long," he said. "But I had the benefit of learning as a kid. Children pick up a new language much faster than adults."

"Don't I know it," she muttered. "I was taking classes in El Paso, and I belong to some parent groups. But it's embarrassing how long it's taking me to learn."

"Stop beating yourself up about it," Carter said. He hated that in addition to everything she'd been dealing with, she felt guilty because she wasn't fluent in sign language after only a few months. "You're doing great."

It didn't take long for Ben to start rubbing his eyes. "Ready for your bath?" Sophia asked, her hands moving as she spoke.

Ben smiled at the sign, clearly understanding her.

Carter knew he should probably leave so as not to disrupt the little one's routine, but he couldn't bring himself to walk away. "Can I help?" He held his breath, fully expecting Sophia to tell him it wasn't necessary. She was used to doing things on her own. She might not appreciate him mucking up the schedule she'd set for their son.

Her answer surprised him. "Sure," she said. "That would be great."

She picked up Ben and waited while Carter got to his feet. "Bathroom's this way," she said. "But first, we'll need to get his jammies and diaper set out."

Carter followed her down the hall, eager to join in this domestic ritual. It was a small thing, but he wanted to help Sophia in any way he could. He needed to spend time with Ben, but he also wanted to spend more time with Sophia.

He'd thought his anger with her would dull his attraction. But that wasn't the case. He was still working through his feelings regarding her decision to wait to tell him about Ben. But watching her with the baby, the way she interacted with him and cared for him, and seeing the love shining in her eyes every time she looked at the boy—it all made her even more irresistible.

They'd shared a few moments today, times when he'd felt they were starting to connect as a family. Maybe they could build on that, make something grow from those promising seeds. It was obvious they still had physical chemistry—the scorching hot kiss at the bar last night had proved that. Could they come together emotionally, as well? Not just to parent Ben, but to have something for themselves?

He ached to touch her, to connect with her on an elemental level. Today had been an emotional roller coaster, for both of them. Maybe, after Ben was asleep, they could spend a little time together. Maybe, just maybe, they could be more than just co-parents.

It was a lot to hope for, but Carter had to try. Sophia had given him a son. Could he convince her to give him a chance, as well?

Chapter 9

It was strange, having someone else help her with Ben's bedtime routine. Sophia was used to doing everything on her own—it was all second nature to her now. But she remembered a time when it had seemed like a never-ending struggle.

Carter didn't seem to have any trouble sliding into their routine. He'd knelt by the side of the tub to wash Ben without complaint, though she knew the position must be uncomfortable for him. She'd stood in the doorway, watching the pair of them. Between washing the baby and signing to him, Carter's hands had never stopped moving. She'd lost count of the number of times Ben had giggled, the sound curling up in her heart like a contented cat.

Even when Ben had started to get fussy, Carter

had handled things like a pro. He'd remained calm, kept his movements slow and measured, and worked to distract the little one until his mood had improved.

Now he stood in the bedroom, cradling a freshly washed, pajama-clad little boy in his arms. Ben was so tired he'd rested his head on his dad's shoulder, a gesture of surrender and trust that brought tears to Sophia's eyes.

"Now what?" Carter asked, turning to her for guidance.

"I usually rock him for a few minutes and sing some lullabies before putting him in the crib," she said.

Something flashed in his eyes. "You sing to him?"

She nodded, feeling suddenly self-conscious. "Yes," she said. "He'll put his hand on my neck, right here." She touched the hollow of her throat, where his little hand usually nestled. "I think he likes the vibrations."

"I'm sure he does," Carter returned softly. "Do you want to take him now?" There was a note of reluctance in his voice, as though he wasn't quite ready to part with the baby.

She shook her head. "You can do the honors tonight." Ben was so relaxed right now, with his eyes drooping and his hands loosely curled in Carter's shirt. It was clear he was getting attached to his father, and she wanted to give them as much time as she could.

"I'll wait in the living room," she told him. She pressed a soft kiss to the top of Ben's head, then walked to the door. A flick of the light switch cast the room in shadows. She stole a final look behind her to see Carter settling into the rocking chair, Ben cradled against him. The sight hit her in the chest, making her breath stutter. There was just something about a man with a baby that was appealing on a primal level.

And the fact that it was her baby and this man? An even more potent combination.

Awareness sparked to life as she walked down the hall. She'd spent the evening watching Carter with Ben, seeing his affection for the baby as he'd played and signed with him. His eagerness to step in and help with Ben had eased a lot of her worries and gone a long way toward making her feel like everything would work out. But seeing his tenderness with her son—*our son*, she reminded herself—had affected her in ways she hadn't anticipated.

She wanted him. Not just as a father for Ben, but physically, the way a woman wanted a man. She'd always found him sexy, had always been drawn to him. But seeing him with the baby, witnessing his care and gentleness as he'd held Ben's tiny body... There was something about the contrast between Carter's leashed strength and the baby's fragility that struck a chord within her, making her body vibrate with desire.

Sophia sank onto the sofa, the fading rays of the sunset bathing the room in shades of gold. Her feelings were probably all one-sided. Oh, sure, the kiss last night had been unambiguous. Carter still wanted her—or at least, he *had*. But now that her secret was out, now that he knew she'd had his baby without telling him for so long, he'd probably never want to touch her again.

She closed her eyes as the weight of sadness settled over her. The hardest part was she'd do it all over again. No, the timing hadn't been ideal—not for her or for Carter. But no matter how many times she dissected her actions and second-guessed her choices, the conclusion was always the same. Telling Carter about the baby right after his accident would have been a mistake.

Should she have told him about Ben sooner? Perhaps after he was born? Probably. But selfishly, she'd wanted the time and space to sort through her own emotions after finding out Ben was deaf. Trying to manage her own grief and Carter's reactions at the same time would have been impossible.

"Doesn't matter," she muttered to herself. What was done was done. Carter knew about everything now. All that mattered was Ben. Sophia would spend the rest of her nights alone if it meant her son would have a relationship with his father.

She wasn't sure how long she sat there. The next thing she knew, the world shifted as a warm touch cradled her head and the scent of sagebrush filled her nose.

Sophia opened her eyes to find Carter's face hovering over her.

He smiled. "Hey," he said softly.

"Hey."

She was on her back, one of his hands on her neck and the other on her shoulder. "Sorry I woke you," he said. "You were asleep, so I wanted to lay you down. Figured it would be more comfortable."

Sophia swallowed, trying to gather her thoughts. It was hard to think with his hands on her, innocent though his touch was. "Thanks," she said lamely.

"Do you want to go to bed?"

"Yes," she said automatically. Then her brain kicked in and she realized it wasn't an invitation. "I mean, no. Not yet." Her cheeks warmed and she pushed herself up. "How did Ben do?"

Carter smiled. "Out like a light," he said proudly.

"Good job," she replied, understanding the feeling. There were days when getting Ben to sleep successfully made her feel like she'd climbed Mount Everest. She didn't have the heart to tell Carter this had been a relatively easy night.

She patted the cushion next to her, inviting him to sit. What was he thinking—and feeling—now that he'd had a few hours to come to terms with the fact that he was a father? Hopefully he'd want to talk to her...

Carter lowered himself to the sofa, a smile still playing on his lips. "Is he always so easy to put to bed?"

Sophia laughed. "Ah, no. Tonight was a good night."

Carter nodded, absorbing this information. "He's truly remarkable." Emotion shone in his eyes as he met her gaze. "I can't believe he's really mine."

Tears stung her eyes. "I know. And I'm sorry I didn't tell—"

He took her hand, cutting off her words. "Don't,"

he rasped, leaning toward her. "I get it. I really do. I can't imagine how hard this past year and a half has been for you. Doing everything alone, on top of your studies…" He shook his head, then squeezed her hand. "You're amazing."

His words washed over her like refreshing summer rain. "I don't know about that," she demurred. His praise made her feel self-conscious; she wasn't anything special. She'd just done what had needed to be done. There hadn't been any other choice.

"*I* know," he said more firmly. He slid his free hand to her jaw, wrapping his fingers around the back of her neck so she had to look at him. "I couldn't have done what you've done. You're incredible. Please believe that."

Sophia nodded, unable to speak. His green eyes drew her in, almost hypnotizing her.

"I'm sorry I wasn't there before," he said gruffly.

She found her voice. "You didn't know."

"Still. I hate that you had to go through everything alone."

She thought about her pregnancy, the doctor's visits. Ben's birth, those first days in the hospital. And all the days after that, filled with visits to specialists and clinics. She wished she could have shared it all with Carter, the good and the bad. But fate had had other plans for them.

"We made it," she said simply.

"I know." His thumb caressed her cheek, making her stomach quiver. "But I'm here now. Let me help you."

Sophia found herself nodding, relief filling her. Carter wasn't like her father. He wanted to know his child, play a role in his son's life. "I'd like that," she whispered.

"I know I haven't known about Ben very long, but I want so much for him."

She smiled. "He's an easy person to love."

Carter's hand dropped from her neck. She immediately missed his touch, had to stop herself from taking his hand and putting it back on her skin.

"Yes," he said. "He is."

So are you, her heart cried silently. What she wouldn't give for the three of them to be a real family!

The thought of family made her think of Margot. "How do you think Margot will react?"

He smiled, clearly imagining the meeting of his son and his sister. "She'll be thrilled. My parents have been pining for grandkids for years. Margot will be excited to find out she's an aunt."

He looked at her then, resolve shining in his eyes. "What time does Ben usually wake up?"

"Around eight," Sophia replied.

"Okay," Carter said. "Margot and I will bring breakfast tomorrow. Will that work for you?"

Sophia nodded, her nerves starting to jangle at the prospect of meeting Carter's sister. "Of course." She wasn't going to keep him away from Ben. And it would be good to meet Margot, to hopefully get some answers to her lingering questions about what it was going to mean for Ben to grow up deaf.

"Great." Carter stood, and Sophia followed suit.

"I'll let you get some rest," he told her, moving for the door.

Sophia followed him, feeling a strange sense of loss. She'd quickly gotten used to having him around today. The house was going to feel empty without him.

He stopped at the door, retrieving his cane, which was leaning on the wall by the jamb. "I'll see you tomorrow?"

She nodded. "Yes. Ben will be so happy to have you back."

Carter smiled. "He's amazing." He paused, looked down at his hands, then back up at her. "Thank you."

Sophia blinked, a bit taken aback. "For what?"

"For taking care of him. For telling me about him. Just…" He trailed off, emotions swirling in his eyes. "For him."

The breath caught in her throat. "Oh." She swallowed hard and tried again. "Of course. You never have to thank me for that." She placed her hand on his arm, needing to touch him, wanting that connection.

Carter stared at her for a moment, his green eyes blazing. Before she could form another thought, he reached for her, pulling her close and capturing her mouth with his own.

The kiss was hot and hard, an outburst of emotion and need that could no longer be contained. Sophia's world spun as Carter held her in place, his passion evident in the tension in his muscles and the tight grip of his hands on her hip and the back of her head. Arousal blazed through her as her own need flared to life. Carter's lips and tongue were insistent, making demands that her body was all too happy to comply with.

This was not the reunion from last night. This kiss was not about attraction and arousal—at least, not entirely. Emotions arced between them as their lips and tongues danced together—anger, yearning, sadness, shock. The maelstrom of feelings that had been swirling and building around them all day was released in this intoxicating moment.

There was a rough edge to Carter that had been lacking the night before, a subtle hardness that betrayed his inner turmoil. He'd said he understood why she'd made the choices she had, but there was a hint of anger in his touch that made it clear he was still upset. He wasn't hurting her—she knew he wouldn't ever do that. She didn't even think the anger was directed at her; it seemed like more of a general frustration with the universe rather than an attempt to punish her. Still, it matched her own mood, her desire to rail against their circumstances. She'd kept things bottled up for far too long, knowing it was futile to rant and scream at the hand of fate. She'd do better to spit against the winds of a hurricane. But in this moment with Carter she felt a kinship, as though they were united against the challenges that loomed ahead.

She threaded her hands through his hair, trying to get even closer. His arm banded around her, pulling her flush to his chest. Her breasts pressed against him, the contact sending zings of sensation to her core.

She felt his arousal grow against her belly. She ran one hand down his back, bringing her palm to rest on the curve of his ass. She squeezed, smiling as he let out a little moan in response. Then she slid her hand around, following the track of his belt until she felt the button of his jeans underneath the buckle.

One of Carter's hands dipped to her neck. Then his mouth followed suit. His lips left a hot trail down the column of her throat, and she bit her bottom lip as his hand found her breast. Her nipples sprang to attention as he palmed the weight of her curves, his teeth nipping lightly at the skin of her shoulder.

"Carter." His name sounded ragged, as though torn from her throat. He felt so good, so hard and hot and heavy against her. She wanted to sink to the floor, feel his weight settle over her as he filled her.

"Please." She was reduced to begging, unable to think or form sentences with his hands on her body. Her fingers fumbled with his belt buckle, hoping he'd get the message. She slid her hand along his length, stroking him through the fabric of his jeans.

He groaned low in his throat and his hips rolled forward in an instinctive response to her touch. "Oh, God," he moaned.

She grinned, loving his reaction. "Nope. Just me." She stood on her toes and nipped his earlobe, earning a husky laugh from Carter.

He cupped her face with his big hands and began kissing her again, stoking the fires of her need. Sophia opened her mouth to suggest they move to the living room—or the dining room, or the kitchen; anywhere with a flat surface, really—when a loud buzzing sound cut her off.

Carter stilled against her, and she could tell he was trying to figure out what was going on. Then he pulled away and sighed. "My phone," he said simply.

He pulled the device from his back pocket and read the screen. He typed out a reply and put it back, then offered her an apologetic smile. "I've got to go."

"Oh." Disappointment speared her. "Right." Her body was still throbbing from his touch, but she had no claim on him. Not really. She might be the mother of his child, but that didn't mean there was anything else between them.

Physical combustibility notwithstanding.

As if sensing her reaction, Carter ran a hand through his hair. "Margot wanted to know where I am. I need to go home and tell her about Ben."

Sophia nodded, knowing he was right. Still, a large part of her wished they could finish what they'd started first.

Carter watched her, his expression conflicted. Did he feel the same way? Was he sorry they'd been interrupted? Or relieved?

"I understand," Sophia said, trying to sound supportive.

He nodded once. "Soph, I'm sorry."

Dread slammed into her. "What for?"

He gestured between them. "I shouldn't have…" He shook his head. "It's been a long day, and our emotions have been running high. I didn't mean to jump on you like that. I know that's not what you need from me. It won't happen again."

On the contrary, screamed her body. "It's okay," she said. "No need to apologize."

He smiled, as though relieved they'd cleared things up. "Great. I'll see you in the morning."

"Yeah." She tried not to take his rejection personally, but disappointment and hurt swirled in her chest. "See you tomorrow," she echoed.

Sophia pasted on a smile as he turned and walked away. She shut the door behind him, then put her back to the wall and slid to the floor.

It seemed that Carter was determined to keep the focus on Ben and off any potential connection between them. She couldn't exactly fault him for wanting to prioritize their son. But it stung to know he didn't want to explore their chemistry, to build a connection with her that went beyond co-parenting.

So much for having it all.

"Finally."

Jake sat up a bit straighter in the front seat of his rental car, his eyes locked on the front door of his grandpa's house. *My house*, he thought bitterly.

The man was leaving, headed for the truck parked in the driveway. Jake focused on the guy's left hand, noting the absence of a wedding band. Satisfaction filled his chest.

I knew it.

She'd lied to him earlier. This wasn't her husband. Just her next mark.

Jake almost felt sorry for the man as he watched him climb into the truck and pull out of the driveway.

Did he have any idea he was being scammed? Should he try to warn him?

No, he decided. If the guy was stupid enough to fall for a pretty face, he deserved what he got.

Jake glanced at his watch, then at the sky. It was only seven thirty. Too early for her to go to sleep. He'd just have to wait longer.

It had taken all his self-control not to bang on the door after his meeting with the lawyer. But after his cold reception earlier, he knew the woman wasn't going to be happy to see him. Better to wait and sneak in after she'd gone to bed. He remembered exactly where his grandfather had kept his safe. It wouldn't take long to find it and extract the original will. And once he had that, he'd be able to build his case that the old man had been out of his head. This was going to take longer than he'd expected, but eventually, he'd win. The house and all its contents would be his, and he could sell everything and start fresh in Vegas.

His phone buzzed from the passenger seat. He picked it up and glanced at the display, frowning at the unfamiliar number.

"Yeah?"

"Jake Porter?"

A kernel of worry formed in his stomach. "Who's this?"

"You're a hard man to find, Jake." The man on the other end of the line sounded friendly enough, but alarm bells started clanging in Jake's head.

"Who am I talking to?"

"Now, is that any way to greet an old friend? It's me, Richard."

A chill skittered down Jake's spine. He injected a note of false cheer into his voice. "Hey, man. How's it going?"

"Oh, you know. The usual. I need you to come by later."

There was only one reason Richard would want to see him, and Jake wasn't about to step inside the man's place of business voluntarily. Not after what Jake had done the last time he'd been there. "What's up?"

"Well, the thing is," Richard said conversationally, "we were going over the security tapes. And I noticed that about a week ago, you were making some pretty sly moves while you were at one of my tables."

Jake could hear Richard blow into the receiver—he was probably smoking—and had a flash of the man sitting in his chair, cigar in hand. He always sat on an elevated platform at the end of the room, lording over his domain.

"I don't know what you're talking about," Jake said. Deny, deny, deny. If he admitted to cheating at one of Richard's games, he'd be in for a world of hurt. Richard's establishment wasn't exactly legal, which meant the man had his own ways of handling trouble.

"I'm sure it's just a misunderstanding," Richard said easily. "That's why I want you to come in. Get this cleared up so we can continue to do business together." He sounded nice enough, but there was a note of steel in his voice that made it clear he wasn't really making a request. This was an order.

"I, uh…I can't right now," Jake said, stammering a bit. "I'm taking care of some personal stuff."

Richard was silent for a moment. When he spoke again, all pretense of friendliness was gone. "Do you really wanna do this the hard way?"

"Look, man, I'm not trying to dodge you. I really am dealing with something. I'll come see you when I get things wrapped up."

"I don't work for you," Richard said smoothly. "I'm not about to operate on your timetable. If your ass isn't in my office tomorrow by three p.m., I'm gonna come looking for you. And you don't want that."

"Richard—"

"You already lost your car," Richard continued, talking over him. "Be a real shame if you were to lose something more…permanent."

Jake's palms started to sweat. "Come on, buddy. I didn't do anything."

"How's your grandpa?"

The question nearly made Jake's heart stop. "What?" he whispered.

Richard laughed. "You think I don't look into the people who come here? I know everything."

"What's my grandpa got to do with this?"

"He's in Texas, right?" Richard continued. He puffed on his cigar. "Maybe I'll send some of my guys down there to check on him. I'm sure you don't see him very often. You're not a very good grandson."

"Okay, Richard," Jake said, unable to hide the tremor in his voice. "You made your point. I'll be there."

"Good." There was a clink of ice cubes as the man

took a drink of something. "I'm only warning you 'cause we've known each other for so long. Don't make me come looking for you."

"I won't," Jake promised.

He ended the call and stared at the phone in his hand, his mind whirling. How had Richard discovered his cheating? He'd been so smooth, or at least he'd thought so. Even the dealer at the table and the other players hadn't suspected anything.

Unless… His stomach dropped as he considered another possibility. Had they been setting him up?

It wasn't the first time he'd cheated at Richard's. Jake didn't do it on a regular basis, just when he absolutely had to win. He was always careful to stick to smaller pots—nothing too outlandish that would trigger a second look. Given the amount of money he'd lost to Richard over the years, he figured they were more than even.

But Richard wouldn't see it that way. And now that he knew Jake had cheated him, he was going to want his pound of flesh.

Literally.

Okay, so new plan. He didn't have time to stick around in Alpine to oust this bitch legally. He had two, maybe three days before Richard's guys would show up. Richard thought he knew everything, but he didn't know Jake's grandfather was dead. Still, he'd send people here to do some damage, and Jake didn't intend to be anywhere near this little town when that happened.

He'd have to break in, get to the safe and take what

was inside. The will should be there, along with a little cash and his grandmother's jewelry. She hadn't had much, but he knew there was a diamond ring and a few other pieces his grandpa had given her over the years. He'd be able to get some money for it all, enough to help him start over someplace new.

And as for the will and the house? He'd just have to fight that fight over the phone. He could mail the will to the lawyer and correspond long-distance. Sooner or later, he'd get his house.

It was close to midnight when Jake decided to make his move. The house had been quiet for hours—the lights were off and the curtains drawn. She had to be asleep.

He climbed out of the car, stretching his aching muscles. Moving stealthily, he walked to the front door. His grandfather had given him a key ages ago. Hopefully she hadn't thought to change the locks…

She hadn't. The key slid in easily, turning smoothly with a flick of his wrist. He stepped inside and shut the door quietly behind him. The last thing he wanted was to wake her and cause a scene.

It still smelled the same. A combination of fabric softener, furniture polish and that medicated cream the old man had rubbed on his joints. A wave of nostalgia hit, and Jake paused in the doorway to the living room, remembering his grandfather on the sofa, a book in his hand.

"Why don't you ever watch TV?" he'd asked once, when he was about ten years old.

Will had smiled. "Everyone's always yelling on that thing," he'd said. "I got my fill of that in the army."

As a child, Jake had been overwhelmed by the number of books on the shelves. It had seemed like they'd gone on forever, a true library right here in his grandpa's home. Now he saw many of them had been taken down, likely packed into the boxes on the floor.

Anger burned through him. She hadn't wasted any time trying to erase his grandfather's presence. And why would she? She'd gotten what she wanted. Hard to move on to your next mark with all the possessions of your first victim lying about, a silent warning to whoever was smart enough to see.

He stole through the house, heading for the kitchen. He'd make sure she got what was coming to her. But in the meantime, he had to find what he needed and scram.

The kitchen hadn't changed, much like the rest of the house. Moonlight shone through the window above the sink, illuminating the green tile on the walls. Jake headed for the far end of the room. Will had kept a small fire safe in the cabinet over the refrigerator. There was no reason for him to have moved it over the years.

He snagged a chair from the small table in the corner and set it softly on the floor in front of the fridge. Then he stepped on the seat, reaching up to open the cabinet.

The door was stuck. He clenched his jaw and pulled as gently as he could. It wrenched free with a scrape that seemed to echo in the otherwise silent room.

Jake held his breath, hoping the woman hadn't heard that. The seconds ticked by, but the house remained silent.

Relieved, he reached inside the dark recesses of the cabinet, expecting to touch the cool, textured surface of the safe. But his hand swiped through empty air.

Alarmed, he stood on his toes to peer inside. Maybe it was just shoved to the back, where he couldn't reach? He tried again. Still no safe.

Panic sprang to life in his chest. Where the hell was it?

He climbed down from the chair and glanced at the doorway. Light—he needed light to see. The safe was around here somewhere, but he didn't have time to stumble around in the dark until he found it.

Jake stuck his head into the hall, looking in the direction of the bedrooms. All quiet on that side of the house. The woman was still sleeping. He could probably risk turning on the overhead light.

He flipped the switch, then crossed the room and climbed back onto the seat of the chair. Craning his head, he looked into the cabinet.

Empty.

The safe was gone.

Fear wrapped around the base of his spine, sending cold tendrils through his limbs. Why had the old man moved it?

And, more important, where had he put it?

Had he gotten rid of it completely? Jake shook his head at the thought. No, Will wouldn't have done that. He'd been a stickler about keeping valuable items in

the safe, so they'd be protected in the unlikely event
the house caught fire. He couldn't imagine his grandfather's thinking on that matter had changed at all.

He'd moved it, then. Perhaps somewhere more easily accessible. That made sense; as the years passed
and Will had grown more unsteady on his feet, he'd
likely wanted to put the safe in a place that didn't require him climbing on a chair to get to it.

The lower cabinets maybe.

Jake climbed off the chair and eyed them, trying
to think like his grandfather. There were a lot of cabinets in this kitchen, and he didn't want to be here any
longer than necessary.

Twenty minutes later, Jake rocked back on his heels
with a disgusted grunt. He'd looked through every
nook and cranny in the room, all to no avail. Even
the pantry had been a dead end.

Where was the damn thing?

The living room.

The bookshelves had panels at the bottom, a cos-
metic feature that he knew doubled as hidden storage.
That had to be where his grandfather had put the safe.

He headed for the living room, so focused on his
goal he tuned out the creaking of the wood floor as
he walked.

The safe was here. He knew it.

And he was going to find it.

Chapter 10

Sophia came awake with a start, her heart pounding. She glanced around, trying to get her bearings. The window was on the wrong side of the room. And was that a desk over there? Where—?

Awareness dawned, and she remembered where she was. Will's house. More specifically, his bedroom.

Hers now.

She relaxed, the tension leaving her muscles as her heartbeat began to slow. She heard the steady rhythm of Ben's breathing from the portable crib on the far side of the room. She focused on the reassuring sound, letting herself drift back into sleep…

A creak from the hallway made her jump. It sounded like a footstep, but surely not. She and Ben were the only ones here. Maybe it was just the house settling.

She slid out of bed and walked to the bedroom door, careful to tread softly so as not to make much noise. There was no chance of disturbing Ben, but if there was actually someone in the house, she didn't want to draw their attention.

Fear made her pause at the door, her hand on the knob. Then she shook her head, dismissing her worry. *It's nothing*, she told herself. She should just go back to bed, but she knew she wouldn't be able to fall asleep again until she'd confirmed the house was safe.

She opened the door, jerking back when she saw light spilling from the kitchen at the other end of the hall. The light had been off when she'd gone to bed. She always made sure to turn off all the lights in the house, so as not to waste electricity. For it to be on now meant only one thing…

Her heart pounded against her ribs and a scrape from the living room nearly made her cry out.

Someone is in the house.

Panic clawed up her throat, threatening to take control. She swallowed hard, determined not to fall apart.

Police. She had to call the police. They'd come and chase off whoever was here.

But first, she had to shut the door. The intruder couldn't know she was awake. She couldn't have them coming back here, searching for her.

Slowly, she shut the door, holding her breath and praying the hinges wouldn't betray her with a squeak. The noise from the living room was growing louder—whoever was in there was growing bolder in their search.

Or more frustrated.

Sophia twisted the lock on the doorknob, then glanced around. The thin wood wouldn't be much of a deterrent to a determined thief, so she grabbed the armchair from the corner and half carried, half dragged it over to shove against the door.

She grabbed her cell phone and glanced at the window. It was halfway up the wall, but wide. It wouldn't be easy to escape that way, especially while holding Ben, but she'd do what she had to in order to keep her baby safe.

"Nine-one-one, what's your emergency?" The operator's voice was calm and smooth, the exact opposite of Sophia's panicked thoughts.

"There's an intruder in my home," she whispered. She crossed to the closet and ducked inside to muffle her voice, keeping the door open so she could still see Ben. Waking him up would only alert the burglar, and she didn't want to spook whoever it was into violence. Better to let the baby sleep peacefully for as long as possible. Hopefully whoever was here would give up and leave soon.

"What's your address?"

Sophia hesitated a second, dredging the information up from the recesses of her brain. She relayed the information, then heard the dispatcher typing.

"Okay, are you someplace safe?"

"I hope so. I'm in my bedroom. I locked the door and have a chair in front of it. But please hurry. My baby is in here with me, and the window is pretty high up, so I don't know if we can get out that way if he tries to break in here."

"The police are on the way, ma'am. I need you to stay on the line with me. Can you do that?"

"Yes," Sophia whispered. Her voice trembled.

"You don't have to talk to me. Just stay with me. Help is almost there."

Sophia nodded, needing to acknowledge the words even though the operator couldn't see. "Thank you," she whispered.

"It's all right," the calm voice said. "Just stay put."

Sophia held her breath, trying to hear past the sound of blood rushing in her ears. Had the noises from the living room stopped? Where was the burglar? Had they left?

A sound from the hall nearly made her heart stop. Footsteps. Drawing near.

"He's coming," she hissed into the phone, her throat so tight she felt like she was being strangled. "He's getting closer."

"Stay hidden," said the operator. "The police are almost there."

But Sophia couldn't cower in the closet while her baby slept in his crib. She flung out her arm, feeling blindly for anything that she could use to defend herself. Her fingers brushed against smooth wood, and she closed her hand around a thick column. Pulling it free, she examined it in the moonlight—a baseball bat. An old one, by the looks of it. There was a large crack down the barrel, but it would have to do.

She set the phone on the floor of the closet and

stepped out, gripping the bat with both hands. She moved softly to the door—she wasn't directly in front, but a bit to the side so she could take a swing if the intruder tried to enter.

The footsteps paused outside the door, and she *felt* him standing there, a malevolent presence only a few feet away. She heard him breathing, felt his indecision as he stood on the other side of the door.

Just go away, she pleaded silently.

For a moment, she thought he would. But to her horror, the doorknob moved slightly.

He was trying to get inside.

Sophia tightened her grip on the bat. There had to be some way of scaring him off, something she could do to keep him from getting to her son.

"The police are on the way," she said loudly, hoping the volume of her voice would disguise her fear. "Get out of here."

She heard him suck in a breath and hoped she'd done the right thing. Her statement would either scare him or spur him into violence. She hoped it was the former.

She couldn't hear him move. For an endless moment, he seemed to be rooted outside the bedroom door. Sophia stepped to the side, positioning herself more fully in front of the crib. She braced to swing the bat, moving one foot slightly behind the other. The bat hit the crib, jostling it.

Ben stirred, letting out a soft cry. *Not now!* she thought, willing him to fall asleep again.

But her son had other ideas. He pushed himself up, rubbed his eyes and let out a loud wail.

The intruder cursed softly. The door vibrated with a loud bang, making Sophia jump. Then she heard footsteps as the man fled down the hall.

She heard the front door slam and dropped to her knees. Unable to walk, she crawled back to the closet and picked up the phone. The operator was speaking in a rapid stream, concern bleeding into his voice.

"Ma'am? Ma'am? Are you all right?"

Sophia put the phone to her ear. "I'm fine," she said. "He's gone. I think." What if he came back? What if he was only trying to trick her into leaving the bedroom?

"Stay where you are," the operator ordered. "The police will be there in less than a minute."

Seconds later, red and blue lights flashed through the bedroom window. She heard the door open again and the officers announce themselves. "They're here," Sophia said, relief washing over her. "What do I do?"

"Wait for them to tell you it's safe. Then you can leave the room and talk to them."

"Thank you," Sophia said, tears in her eyes. She'd never meet the voice on the other end of the line, but she felt immense gratitude for the man's kindness.

"You'll be all right now," he said. "Take care of yourself."

She ended the call just as there was a knock on the door. "Ma'am? Are you in there?"

"Yes," she called out. "I just need a minute to pull the chair away."

She turned on the bedroom light—no sense in

keeping the place dark, now that Ben was awake—and managed to drag the chair to the side. She unlocked the door, then picked up Ben and opened it.

Two uniformed officers stood in the hall, their expressions concerned. "Is the baby okay?"

"He's fine," Sophia said. "Just unhappy about being awake."

"Is there anyone else in the room with you?" one of the officers asked.

She shook her head. "Just us."

The other man nodded. "The rest of the house is empty. Can you please come with us and tell us what happened?"

Sophia nodded, adjusting her hold on Ben as she followed the men down the hall. As they passed by the living room, she gasped.

All the decorative panels on the front of the bookcases had been pried off, and the contents had been strewn about the room. The books she'd already boxed up were now in piles on the floor, and those that remained on the shelves were askew, as though the intruder had been searching behind them.

"I take it the room doesn't normally look like this?"

She shook her head mutely.

"Can you take a look at the kitchen?"

She followed the officers into the kitchen, bracing for the worst.

All the cabinet doors were open, various items on the floor, on the counters, everywhere but inside. The pantry door was open, the scene inside matching the rest of the room.

"I know it's hard to determine," one officer said. "But can you tell if anything is missing?"

"I—I'm not sure," Sophia stammered. "I've only lived here a few days."

The officers frowned and exchanged a look. Haltingly, she told them how she'd inherited the house from Will and had just started going through the contents.

"Let's sit down," one of the men suggested. He led her to the dining room and pulled out a chair for her. She sank onto the seat, noting the china hutch on the wall had been subject to a search, as well. Nothing appeared to be broken, but whoever had been here had clearly been looking for something.

Ben, having forgotten his earlier displeasure, began to squirm in her arms and make the sign for *down*. She tightened her hold on him, needing to feel his warm little body against her own to know he was truly safe. Her son let out a cry of protest at this, then redoubled his efforts to escape her grasp.

"Here," said one of the officers, reaching out for the baby. "Why don't you let me take him into the other room while you tell my partner what happened?"

The gesture made Ben shrink against her for a second. But apparently the little one realized this man was his only ticket down. He reached for him, grunting with effort.

She watched her arms move, as though under someone else's command, and she lifted up the baby so the officer could hold him. "Thank you," she said, feeling a little numb. The man turned to go, and she blurted out, "He's deaf."

The officer paused, then glanced back at her with his eyebrows raised in surprise. "So, you know, he won't respond to you when you talk," she added lamely.

"That's okay," the man said. "I bet he'll like a teddy bear, though. Come on, little man. I've got a friend in my trunk I think you'll want to meet." He carried Ben out of the room, smiling at the boy.

"Ben," she said softly. "His name is Ben." Then she turned to the other officer with a slight frown. "You keep a teddy bear in the trunk?"

The man nodded. "Several, actually. Helps when we have calls involving kids."

"Oh." It was something she'd never thought of, never had reason to consider. "That's…nice." Her mind whirled, her thoughts jostling together as her emotions vied for attention. She wasn't sure how to feel; her brain knew she was safe now, but her body was still in fight-or-flight mode. The contrast was unsettling.

The officer watched her, his eyes kind. "I know you've had quite a scare tonight," he said gently. "Can you please explain what happened?"

She nodded, then started talking, telling him what she could. "I don't know what time he broke in," she murmured. "I only know it looked like he was here for a while, given everything…" She trailed off, waving her arm around to encompass the disarray. She shivered at the thought of him pawing through the house while she slept. Even though she hadn't been here long and didn't have an emotional attachment to Will's things, she still felt violated. Her safety, and the safety of her son, had been put in jeopardy.

"There doesn't appear to be any damage to the front door. Do you know how he got in?"

She shook her head. "I heard the door slam when he left, so I assume that's what he used."

"And you're certain the intruder was male?"

Sophia blinked, considering the question for the first time. Could it have been a woman in the house? No, that didn't feel right…

"I never saw him," she admitted slowly. "But I do think it was a man. There was something about the sounds he made when he moved. And I think he punched the bedroom door before he left."

A memory pinged in her mind, and she struggled to unearth it. Someone else had lashed out like that, in the recent past.

The answer came to her with a flash that made her sit up straighter in the chair. "Jake," she said, practically shouting the name.

The officer frowned, his pen stalling on the notepad in front of him. "Who?"

"Jake Porter." Sophia leaned forward, telling him about the man's earlier visit, and the way he'd kicked the wall after she'd shut the door and refused to let him come inside. "He told me he's Will's grandson, but I don't know if that's true. I left a message for Will's attorney, but he hasn't returned my call."

"So you think he's the one who broke in tonight?"

"Who else could it be?" she asked. "He was upset that I'm here because he thinks this should all be his. Maybe he decided to break in and take something tonight. He might even have a spare key, which would explain why there's no damage to the door."

"That's definitely possible," the officer said, scribbling madly. "Can you tell me what he looks like?"

Sophia narrowed her eyes, picturing the man's face as she described his features. The more she thought about it, the more certain she was that he was the one who'd done this.

"All right." The officer closed his notepad and stood. "Thanks for your help tonight, ma'am. We'll be on the lookout for him."

Sophia got to her feet and hugged herself. "Do you think he'll come back?"

The man frowned. "I can't make any guarantees, but I think you're safe for the rest of the night. We'll step up patrols in this area and do a few drive-bys while it's still dark. Is there someplace you can go so you'll feel safer?"

She shook her head. "No." Her aunts would panic if she showed up in the middle of the night. Now that the threat was over, she just wanted to sleep and not have to worry about managing someone else's emotions. "But I do have a friend I can call."

The officer nodded. "Be sure to get those locks changed tomorrow. If you need anything else, feel free to call me directly." He withdrew a business card from his pocket and handed it to her. "Alpine's not that big," he told her with a smile. "We'll find this guy and he won't bother you anymore."

"Thank you," Sophia said, gratitude welling inside her chest. They walked into the living room together, and she saw the other officer kneeling on the floor, entertaining Ben with a stuffed bear.

"All set?" the man asked when he caught sight of them.

"Yep," his partner replied. He tapped the pocket that held his notepad. "Got a suspect description. Let's get to work."

"Right on." The man passed Ben the bear, then ruffled his hair gently. "Get back to sleep, little man," he said, holding his hands to his cheek and tilting his head in a pantomime of sleep. He glanced up at Sophia. "Is that how you do it?"

She didn't have the heart to tell him differently. "Close enough," she said, smiling. "Thanks for trying."

"Sure thing." He walked past her, and the pair paused at the doorway.

"Call us if you notice anything is missing," said the officer who'd taken her statement.

"I will," she said. "And thank you again."

"Anytime, ma'am," said the man who'd played with Ben. He touched his brow in a small salute and the two cops walked out.

She followed them, flipping the lock into place behind them. Then she returned to the living room and sat on the floor, feeling overwhelmed by the mess.

Ben crawled over to her and climbed into her lap.

She snuggled him close, dropping her nose to his hair to inhale his sweet baby scent. Some of the tension left her muscles as she held him. He was safe. She was safe. It was enough for now.

He rubbed his eyes with small fists. "Let's try this again," she said, picking him up. At his sound of protest, she bent down and retrieved the teddy bear the officer had given him. Then she returned to the bedroom and rocked him for a few minutes. His body went limp against her, and she placed him in the crib. Then she stood there for a moment, looking down at his sleeping form.

The shakes hit her so fast she nearly fell over. She dropped to the ground, landing hard on her bottom. She drew up her legs, then rested her chin on her knees and gripped her shins tight, trying to control her quaking. But it was no use. Her teeth chattered together as though she was in a blizzard and not sitting on the bedroom floor. Clenching her jaw, she unfolded and crawled over to the bed, reaching for the phone she'd dropped on the mattress when the police had arrived.

This is ridiculous, she thought, clutching the phone with both hands. *I'm fine. We're fine. He's gone.* But no matter how many times she told herself she and Ben were safe, her body refused to acknowledge logic.

Feeling simultaneously foolish and desperate, she punched in Carter's number. Maybe just hearing his voice would be enough to calm her down. But as soon as he answered, his deep voice rumbling over the line, she broke down.

"Can you please come over?"

Carter planted one arm on the mattress and pushed up, using his other hand to flip over his pillow for what felt like the millionth time that night. Falling asleep should have been easy; he was tired, both physically and mentally. Today had been emotionally draining, to put it mildly. His body needed rest and his mind needed a break to recharge so he could continue to process the fact that he was now a father.

Fortunately, his dad had been a supportive part of his life from the beginning. Frank Donaghey was a hard worker who had worked tirelessly to provide for his family. And he'd always had time for Carter and Margot, making sure they knew how much he loved them and how important they were to him. Carter had known he was one of the lucky ones—not all of his friends had had such a positive relationship with their fathers—but now that he had a child of his own, he was even more appreciative of the good example Frank had set.

He hadn't known about Sophia's childhood, that she'd had to grow up without her dad around. The revelation had stunned him and left him even more impressed by her strength. If anyone knew the challenges of single motherhood, it was her. Yet she'd chosen to forge ahead, despite her uncertainties regarding his role in their baby's life.

It was amazing, the amount of stress she'd handled

over the past year and a half. But she didn't need to shoulder it all by herself anymore. Now that he knew about Ben, Carter was going to do everything in his power to help her. He still felt a little shell-shocked when he thought about the baby, but he was determined to be a true father to his son, not a drive-by dad or a part-time parent.

It would be hard—that much he knew. Logistically speaking, they'd have to determine where they'd live. Was Sophia going to stay in Alpine, or go back to El Paso after she sold the house? He wanted to be nearby so he could help, but what would she think of that? She was so used to doing everything alone, she might not appreciate him stepping in. Maybe she'd see it as interference, rather than assistance.

And what about their jobs? She was still in graduate school, but that wouldn't last forever. Where did she see herself once she'd graduated? Carter's own career prospects were uncertain. Physically, he didn't think he'd be able to return to regular patrols in Big Bend. His body just wasn't the same, and while he'd made great strides in his recovery, there were certain things he simply couldn't do anymore. He didn't want to leave the park service, but he wasn't sure he could stay at Big Bend if it meant sitting behind a desk. He loved the park too much to cut himself off from it.

Then there was Ben to consider. His deafness meant he'd need accommodations at school, and Carter knew some districts had more resources than others. They'd have to work together to make sure Ben got what he needed. And they were already at odds on one of those decisions.

Hopefully meeting Margot would help Sophia see that Ben didn't need a cochlear implant. He hated the idea of the baby going through surgery, not to mention all the challenges he'd face trying to adjust to this new sensory input. He also didn't want to do anything that would make Ben feel that he was somehow broken. He was too young to draw that conclusion now, but as he got older, he might feel that he'd been given an implant in an attempt to "fix" him.

And those were only the things Carter had come up with in the past few hours. There were likely millions more decisions to be made, things he had no way of anticipating. He and Sophia would have to work together, to act as a team going forward.

There were things she needed from him—his help, his partnership. What she did not need was him pawing at her like a randy teenager, the way he had earlier tonight while saying goodbye.

He hadn't meant to kiss her. Certainly hadn't meant to pull her close and put his hands on her body. Thank God for Margot's text; he'd been about ready to drag Sophia down to the floor and have his way with her, and she definitely deserved better than that.

Carter sighed, his skin tingling at the memory of her searing touch. She hadn't pulled away from him. In fact, she'd matched his rising intensity with enthusiasm. So maybe his attraction wasn't all one-sided. And really, why couldn't they kill two birds with one stone? They were adults—surely they could handle being parents and exploring their connection at the same time. There was no law that said it had to be one or the other.

But…doubts crept in, darkening the edges of his thoughts. What if they did give things a try, only to crash and burn? If they wound up hurting each other, that would only make things harder for Ben. Once upon a time, Carter wouldn't have hesitated to seize this second chance with Sophia. But now that their son was in the picture, his needs took priority over Carter's baser urges.

He rolled over with a sigh, wishing he could simply shut off his brain and sleep. Maybe a shot of whiskey would help him relax…

The phone buzzed on the bedside table, distracting him from his insomnia. He grabbed it, and his heart thumped hard when he saw the name on the screen. *Sophia.*

Was she tossing and turning, too, trying to figure out exactly what tonight's kiss had meant and where they should go from here?

"Hello?" As he answered the call, a jolt of worry shot down his spine. She might simply be calling to chat. Or maybe something had happened to Ben.

He'd barely gotten the word out before she started speaking. "Can you please come over?"

He could tell by the sound of her voice she was upset. "Is the baby okay? Is something wrong?"

"He's fine," she said. But it was clear she was crying.

Carter was out of bed and grabbing his pants before she could get the next sentence out. "Can you please come over?" she repeated. "Someone broke in earlier, and I don't feel safe anymore."

"What?!" He tugged a shirt over his head and jammed his feet into shoes. Grabbing his wallet, cane and keys, he raced for the door as fast as he could move. "I'm on my way. Are the police there?"

"No," she said. "They left a few minutes ago. The doors are locked and there's no real damage, but…" She trailed off, sniffling. "Maybe I'm just being paranoid."

"Absolutely not," Carter retorted, climbing into his truck. He felt like he'd been doused in ice water, and his stomach was twisted into a giant knot in his belly. "I'd say you're worried for good reason. Would you rather stay at my place?"

Sophia was quiet for a few seconds, clearly considering his offer. "No," she said finally. "I just got Ben back to sleep, and I don't want to disturb him again. The police don't think whoever did this is going to come back tonight, and they're going to do some patrols of the neighborhood, just to make sure." Her voice grew stronger as she spoke. "Like I said, I'm probably overreacting. In fact, maybe you should just stay home. I shouldn't have bothered you."

"Like hell," Carter growled, punching the gas to make it through a stale green light. Anxiety was a little devil on his shoulder, whispering in his ear to go faster, before it was too late. "I'll be there in two minutes. I'm not leaving you and Ben alone after a break-in."

"Don't speed," Sophia admonished him. "We're safe. There's no need to rush."

"Yes, ma'am," he said, barely slowing for the final

turn onto her street. Better to appease her than have her worry. "I'm about to pull into your driveway. Get ready to unlock the door."

She sputtered in surprise as he parked and cut the engine. Only when she opened the door and he saw for himself that she was safe did he hang up the phone.

He stepped inside and gathered her into his arms, pressing her against his chest. "Are you all right?"

She hugged him back, her arms snaking around his waist and squeezing. She laid her head over his heart, and as he felt her steady breathing against his chest, he began to relax.

"I'm fine. We're fine," she said quietly.

He dropped his head, his nose only inches from her hair. A deep breath drew her scent into his lungs, filled his head with her, chasing away the last of his fears. "And Ben?"

"He's asleep again. He would have slept through the whole thing, but I accidentally bumped his crib and the movement woke him up."

"Can I…? I need to see him." He trusted Sophia, knew she wouldn't lie to him about Ben's safety. But he needed to see the baby for himself.

She smiled up at him, understanding in her brown eyes. "Of course," she said softly. "Come on—I'll show you."

She took his hand and led him down the hall into the bedroom. There was a portable crib set up against one wall, and as Carter approached, he could see the little one stretched out on his stomach, his head turned to the side. His mouth was slack, one small hand curled up near his lips and the other spread flat against the mattress. He was the very picture of relaxation, and seeing him whole and unharmed unwound the knots of tension in Carter's heart.

They left the room together, keeping the door cracked so they could hear if the baby woke up. The living room was a mess, but Carter ignored the signs of the break-in. He sat on the sofa and pulled Sophia down next to him, keeping her hand in his.

"Tell me everything."

She took a deep breath and began, starting from when she'd woken up to when she'd called him. His heart began to pound as she related the details. Things could have gone so differently tonight! If she hadn't heard the intruder, hadn't called the police, he probably would have come into the bedroom while she and Ben slept. If she hadn't spoken up and scared him off, he might have tried to force his way inside. And what then? What would he have done to her, to their baby? Just the thought of anything happening to the two of them turned Carter's legs to jelly, and he was glad to be sitting down.

At the same time, anger burned through him. His child had been put in danger tonight. His woman, too, though Sophia might object to that label. Too bad—she was his, like it or not. They might never have a romantic relationship, but she was always going to be part of his life and he would always feel a need to provide for her and help her. Maybe he was old-fashioned, maybe the caveman part of his brain was taking over, but she and Ben belonged to him. As long as there was breath in his body, he would do anything to keep them safe.

She shivered next to him, clearly upset as she spoke. He put his arm around her and pressed a kiss to the top of her head.

"It's okay," he soothed, stroking her upper arm. "I'm here now. I won't let anyone hurt you or Ben."

"I think he has a key."

That got his attention. He paused midstroke, digesting this bit of news. "What makes you say that?"

She told him about Jake Porter, the man who claimed to be Will's grandson. The way he'd visited her earlier, his displeasure at finding her in the house.

"We'll change all the locks," Carter declared. "I'll go first thing in the morning, as soon as the hardware stores open. We can even put some extra locks on, as additional deterrent. And I want you and Ben to stay with me until he's apprehended." His apartment wasn't large, but they would make it work. She could have his bed and he'd take the couch. The discomfort was a small price to pay for knowing she and the baby were safe.

"Oh, no," she said. "We can't do that."

Carter drew back and stared at her, blinking in confusion. This was a no-brainer. Someone was out there with an agenda, and it was clear they were after something inside this house. Changing the locks was a good first step, but he doubted the intruder was going to be put off so easily. Unless he missed his guess, this guy was going to come back. And the next time, he might not be content to simply ransack a few rooms.

"Sophia," he began slowly. Carter needed her to understand his worry, but he didn't want to terrify her. "If Jake really is the one who broke into the house tonight, he's after something. The fact that he was about to come into the bedroom means he didn't find it out here."

The color drained from her face as realization dawned. "Oh. I didn't think of it like that."

Carter took her hand. "I'm not trying to be alarmist here, but he's probably going to try again."

"But…the locks," she said weakly.

"I doubt he'll let new locks stop him," Carter replied. "And given the way he acted with you before, it's probably only going to escalate. If he finds you here, he might hurt you."

"I don't have what he's looking for!" Fear laced her tone and he could tell his words were making an impact.

"I know that, and you know that. But do you think he'll believe you?"

She shook her head. "No," she said dully.

"So you'll come stay with me?"

She nodded. "Only to keep Ben safe," she clarified, as though she needed to justify her decision.

"Thank you," he said.

"I have to keep working here during the day, though," she added. "There's so much left to sort through, and now I have even more work since he made such a mess here and in the kitchen."

Carter's chest constricted at the reminder that Sophia was only in town for a short while. They had so much to discuss, so many details to arrange. It was the kind of thing that could take a lifetime, if they both wanted it to.

He swallowed his disappointment and nodded. "I'll help you," he offered. He hated the idea of hastening her departure from Alpine, but he'd promised himself he was going to do whatever was needed to make Sophia's and Ben's lives easier. If that meant helping her sort through all the stuff in this house and getting the place ready to sell, so be it.

"That would be great," she said on a sigh of relief.

It wouldn't be so bad, he realized. They'd get to spend time together, and he'd be around to protect her and the baby, if the intruder tried anything again.

Carter was under no illusions about his physical abilities. The accident had taken a lot from him, but he could still handle himself fairly well. Besides, all he'd need to do was keep the two of them safe long enough for them to get away. He could definitely do that, if it came down to it.

"That makes me feel so much better," she continued, smiling up at him. "I thought this was going to take at least a month, but with you and Leah helping, we should be able to get it done in a couple of weeks."

"So you can go back to El Paso," he finished. Just saying the words made him die a little inside, but he tried not to let it show. Sophia had enough to worry about already; he wasn't going to add to her stress by trying to guilt-trip her into staying longer.

"Well, yeah," she said, sounding a little awkward. "I do need to finish school."

"Of course." Carter pasted on a smile. "Come on," he said, changing the subject. "You should go to sleep. I'll take the couch."

"Oh. Um." Sophia blushed, a pretty shade of pink spreading across her cheeks. "Actually, I was wondering… That is, if you don't mind…"

Carter's libido perked up at her response, but he forcibly tamped down the inappropriate reaction and focused on her eyes, which shone with vulnerability in the lamplight.

"Would you please sleep in the bed with me?" she finally said. "I'd feel better knowing you're close."

"Absolutely," he replied. Truth be told, he'd feel better, as well, knowing he was within arm's reach of the two of them. The police were probably right— whoever had broken in tonight wasn't going to try again in the few remaining hours of darkness. But Carter wanted to stay close, to watch over her and Ben to ensure they were really safe.

They stood together, and Sophia turned off the lights. Together, they walked through the shadows to check the locks on the front door. "Want me to put a chair here?" he offered. He spoke softly, though there was no chance of his voice disturbing Ben. There was just something about the moment that demanded a whisper.

Sophia nodded, and he caught the flash of relief on her lovely face. He walked to the living room and re-turned with one of the chairs, angling it so it fit under the door handle. If anyone tried to get in through here, the chair would jam against the door and prevent it from opening.

"Now the back door," he said. She followed him as he repeated the procedure there, helping him position the chair just so.

He straightened, catching her staring at him in the moonlight coming in through the window. "That's the best I can do right now," he said, wishing there was some other action he could take to fortify the house.

"It's enough," she told him, gratitude shining in her eyes. "Thank you."

"Anytime." Driven by impulse, he tucked a strand of hair behind her ear. She reached for him, but stopped herself before touching him. A look of regret crossed her face. "We should get some sleep," she said, pulling back her hands.

No! his body shouted. Sleep was overrated, especially when something else was being offered. But after the scare she'd had earlier, Sophia needed to rest. It wouldn't be right to suggest anything physical right now. If and when they did sleep together again, he wanted them to have clear heads. Right now, both their minds were still fuzzy with the emotions of the day. And while sex would certainly help them both feel better, he didn't want her to have any regrets in the morning.

"You're right," he said. She walked past him and he turned to follow her down the hall, into the bedroom where their son was resting peacefully.

Carter slid into bed next to Sophia, careful not to

touch her. He had the best of intentions, but he was only human. Given the events of the day—and more specifically, of the past hour or so—he didn't think he'd be getting much sleep. Adrenaline swirled in his body, seeking some kind of outlet. Since there was nothing to fight, and he wasn't going to try to, uh, find release with Sophia, he was left staring at the ceiling.

But as he felt her relax next to him and heard the rhythm of her breathing change as she sank into slumber, a calmness stole over Carter. Here in the dark, in the stillness of the house, he could hear the soft breaths of his son and feel Sophia's warmth close by. There was something so profound about those simple things and the absolute trust they represented. Sophia had called him. She'd been scared and she'd called him to make it better. And she'd wanted him to stay close, to sleep in her bed. It was enough to make him feel ten feet tall and bulletproof.

My family, he thought, as sleep tugged at the edges of his mind. *They're mine.*

It was more than that, though, he realized as he drifted off. They were his; that much was true.

And he was theirs.

Jake paced the hotel room, anger and disappointment swirling in a toxic brew low in his belly.

Where was the damn safe?

His grandfather had been a creature of habit, a man you could set your watch by. Coffee and toast at 8:30 a.m. sharp. Grocery store on Wednesday afternoons, post office on Friday mornings. Never changed, always constant.

So why had he moved the safe?

The woman's face flashed in his mind. Of course. He'd probably told her where it was, so she'd know in case she ever needed to get inside. The same way he'd shown Jake, back when Jake was still a kid. The old man was nothing if not prepared for every eventuality.

Naturally, the bitch had moved it once she'd taken over.

But did she know what was inside? Had she bothered to look? Or had she forgotten, feeling secure enough in the house that she wasn't worried about some old papers?

Either way, she had to know where it was.

"She'll never tell me," he muttered. Once she knew he wanted it, she'd most likely get inside and destroy the will. Couldn't leave anything that might challenge her claim, after all. Jake clenched his jaw. He'd have to go back through the house again, this time checking all the rooms if he wanted to have a chance of finding the safe.

It had to be in the bedroom. That was the only place he hadn't checked. The kitchen, dining room and living room had all been disappointments. There wasn't any storage in the laundry room, and he doubted his grandfather or the woman would put the safe in the bathroom. So that left the bedroom, or perhaps the closet. Either way, he had to get inside.

He needed some time to go through everything without interruptions. But he didn't know her schedule, and with Richard's threat hanging over his head, he didn't exactly have time to learn it. No more stakeouts for him; he was going to have to make a move, and fast.

His mind whirred, forming possibilities and discarding them just as quickly. How could he get her out of the house for a long period of time? What could he do to keep her distracted and away?

A thin wail sounded from somewhere nearby, grabbing his attention. That was the problem with these cheap motels: the walls were so thin…

Lightning struck, and for a second, Jake forgot to breathe. "Oh, yes," he said softly. "How perfect."

He'd heard something when he'd been standing in the hall outside the bedroom door. She hadn't been alone in that room.

She had a baby with her.

A baby he was willing to bet she'd walk to the ends of the earth for.

"You won't have to go that far," he said, smiling sinisterly as the plan began to take shape in his mind. "But I'll definitely lead you on a chase."

It wasn't ideal, and it would require a fair bit of luck. But he had no other options.

That baby was the key to his survival.

And he was going to use it.

Chapter 11

Sophia woke early as the dawn light gently tapped on the bedroom window. She lay there for a moment, listening to the sounds of her son and Carter. Both of them were breathing in a relaxed and regular manner.

Slowly, she turned her head to look at the man beside her. Carter was sleeping on his back, his face in profile and one hand resting on his chest. Even in the pale gray light, he was beautiful, though he probably wouldn't appreciate the description.

She'd always found him attractive. There was something about his dark hair, green eyes, ready smile and solid build that called to her. The months apart had done little to dampen his appeal. Even the accident hadn't changed things.

He'd kicked off the covers sometime during the

night. She ran her gaze along the long lines of his body, lingering on the silvery scars that marred his skin. When he'd told her the number of surgeries he'd had, her jaw had dropped. It still blew her mind he'd survived, given all the damage he'd sustained from the fall. She knew from their conversations he was still adjusting to his physical limitations, but there was no doubt in her mind he'd do whatever it took to get back to normal again. His body might be healing, but his willpower was stronger than ever.

Her hand stole closer, itching to touch him. It had been so long since she'd felt the warmth of sexual attraction to a man. During her pregnancy, she hadn't wanted anyone to touch her. After the delivery, she'd been so focused on healing and learning more about Ben's condition that she hadn't had time for any physical urges. Once she'd come to terms with Ben's deafness and had come up with a plan for learning sign language, she'd finally been able to give a little thought to her personal life. But she'd taken a long look around and realized the list of prospective dating candidates was nonexistent. There wasn't anyone she trusted to be around her son. Furthermore, whoever she was with would have to embrace both her and Ben, which meant he'd have to learn how to talk to her son. It was hard enough for her to learn sign language. There wasn't exactly a crowd of men eager to learn ASL so they could interact with a baby.

But there was one man who already knew sign language, and whom she did trust. And while she was thrilled that Carter seemed excited by the prospect of fatherhood, she wasn't so sure how he felt about her.

Yes, those kisses had made her toes curl. But from their conversations, she knew he'd been so focused on recovery that he hadn't had time for a relationship. Maybe he was reaching out to her because he had his own itch to scratch and she was the closest warm body?

With a sigh, she slipped from the bed and headed for the bathroom. As she washed her hands, she looked at herself in the mirror, taking stock of her sleep-tangled red hair, the dark circles under her eyes and her pale skin. Definitely not her best look. But she just couldn't bring herself to care.

Maybe they should just have sex and get it over with, clear the air so they could focus on other issues. But would she be okay knowing Carter was only using her for temporary relief?

It'd be better than nothing, she thought, tiptoeing back into the bedroom. After all, it wasn't like the pleasure would be all one-sided. She'd enjoy the experience, as well, and it would definitely be a nice distraction.

She stood at the edge of the bed for a moment, taking the opportunity to study him again. He wasn't as muscular as he'd been in the past, but his strength was still there, his body still hard in all the right places. Sophia closed her eyes, remembering how it felt to be pressed against him, the warm, solid wall of his chest under her cheek. There was an energy to his touch that she found intoxicating, a leashed power that made her feel like he was frantic to put his hands on her, but that he was holding himself back so as not to hurt her. It was a potent combination that made her long to test the limits of his steely self-control. He'd let go with her once before, and it had been amazing. Would they have that same magic a second time?

Sophia carefully climbed back into bed, trying not to disturb Carter. She should probably just file these thoughts under "questions best left unanswered." If it had just been her, she'd jump at the chance to give things with Carter another try. But there was Ben to consider. If they got involved and it ended badly, Carter might decide to leave, the way her own father had. The last thing she wanted was for her son to grow up without his father. If that meant keeping her distance from Carter, so be it.

She rolled onto her side, determined to go back to sleep. Ben wouldn't wake up for a few more hours, and she needed the rest. But no sooner had she closed her eyes than the mattress shifted next to her, and Carter's arm draped over her waist.

Before she could speak, he pulled her close, her back against his chest, her bottom against his groin. He was warm from sleep, his body like a furnace blazing against her.

Sophia's heart stuttered against her ribs as Carter slid his big hand up her belly and found her breast. He squeezed gently, his hips rocking against her as he nuzzled her neck.

Her body melted, heat pooling in her core as she felt his arousal grow. She should stop him. They should talk about this, but, oh, God, he rocked against her again and her brain lost the ability to form coherent thoughts.

She reached back, putting her hand on his head as he licked a trail down the side of her neck. She shivered as the cool air hit her skin. "Carter?" Maybe he was still asleep? Maybe he didn't know what he was doing?

"Sophia," he responded. There was a raspy note to his voice that stroked her like a caress.

"Are you awake?" It was a silly question, but she had to know. Were they going to talk about this or simply let go and just feel?

Carter stilled behind her. "That depends," he rumbled in her ear. "Do you want me to be?"

He was giving her a choice, letting her decide how to proceed. They could stop altogether, or they could get lost in each other, with no promises or expectations for the future.

For one interminable moment, she hung between the two options. What was the best choice? What should she do?

Then her heart took control, overriding her brain and her seemingly endless list of worries. She pressed back against Carter, threading her fingers through his hair as she arched into his embrace.

"No," she said. "We should both stay asleep for this." She was tired of thinking, tired of stressing about everything and every possible outcome. It was exhausting, trying to see into the future all the time. Right now, she just wanted to *feel*. To let her mind go and lead with her body. Her worries would wait. But this moment with Carter, this opportunity to connect with him again, wasn't going to last forever.

He chuckled in her hair, his hands resuming their slow exploration of her body. "I was hoping you'd say that. What about Ben?"

"He won't get up for a while," she replied, biting her lip as he slid his hand under her nightshirt. The drag of his calluses triggered a wave of goose bumps, and her nipple puckered against his palm.

"Thank God." Carter's breath was hot along her neck, his hips thrusting more forcefully against her bottom. He nipped her shoulder, and the possessive gesture sent a zing to her core.

Sophia pressed against him, reaching back with her hand to clutch his hip. She squeezed tightly, loving the feel of him moving against her. But there was too much fabric between them—she needed to feel his skin against her own.

She fumbled at the waistband of his boxer-briefs, unable to get a good grip from this angle. Before she could so much as move, Carter shifted and rolled her until she was flat on her back, his hand under her shirt pinning her to the mattress.

"Allow me," he said with a grin. In one smooth move, he hooked his thumbs into the waistband of her panties and tugged them off her body, exposing her to his gaze.

Sophia didn't have time to be stunned. One second, she felt the cool air on her heated skin. The next second, Carter was there, kissing her intimately, licking and tasting her.

Her hands fisted in the sheets as pleasure rolled over her in waves. Her breath stalled in her chest and she arched her back, the sensations almost too much to bear. She looked down, and the sight of Carter on his knees, his face between her legs, sent her over the edge. She moaned as her body responded, her hips jerking reflexively against him as her core clenched, aching to be filled.

Carter slowly worked his way up her body. "If we were awake," he said softly, "I'd tell you how long I've wanted to do that."

Sophia smiled, warmth spreading through her limbs. She reached for him, bringing him in for a kiss. "Don't deny yourself on my account," she replied. "I'd hate for you to feel deprived."

He laughed softly and kissed her again. She pulled up her knees, then put her feet on his hips and pushed his underwear down his legs. He pulled back, blinking in surprise.

"Nice trick," he said dryly.

She grinned. "Wasn't sure it would work." She planted her feet on the mattress and shifted, bringing her body in contact with his arousal.

He sucked in a breath through his teeth. "Condoms?"

"I've got an IUD," she said. She'd had it implanted at her six-week postbirth checkup, wanting something that would lighten her periods so she'd have one less thing to worry about. She hadn't actually thought she'd need it for birth control, but now she was glad for its multiple uses.

Relief flashed in Carter's eyes. She reached between them, guiding him into place. He rocked forward slowly, entering her with a gentleness that bordered on reverence.

Once they were fully joined, he looked down at her, emotions swirling in his green eyes. "I've missed you so much," he whispered.

Tears stung her eyes, and she blinked to clear them. "Same here," she said. "I never stopped thinking about you."

He began to move then—short, shallow thrusts that grew deeper and harder as the seconds ticked by. Sophia wrapped her legs around his waist and gripped his shoulders, surrendering to the pleasure. Her heart swelled in her chest as he moved against her. This was more than just sex. This was a communion between two souls, a reunion of hearts that had been apart for too long. She didn't know what the future held in store for them, but in this moment, she knew they were one.

Carter's rhythm changed, his pace growing more frantic as he drew closer to his release. Sophia clenched around him, urging him on. His hips jerked against her once, twice, and then he stilled, panting above her as his own pleasure rolled through him. She felt him throb inside her, spent. He came to rest on top of her, his body a solid weight that made her feel deliciously feminine.

She ran her hand up and down the valley of his spine as aftershocks zinged through them both. Time stretched as they lay entwined, bodies growing cooler as the heat of arousal and exertion dissipated.

Sophia could have stayed like this forever, feeling Carter's heart beat against her own, wrapped up in him. But all too soon, he shifted, rolling off her and onto his side.

"That was…" He trailed off, as though words failed him.

"Yeah," she said, understanding perfectly. Whatever else was going on, the chemistry between them was alive and well. Maybe they could build on that, use it as a starting point for everything else.

She glanced at the clock and groaned. Ben would be up in about forty minutes. As much as she wished she could stay in bed with Carter all day, she couldn't ignore the real world forever.

"What's wrong?" He reached for her, pulling her close once more.

"Ben will be up soon. I need to take a shower." But she made no move to get out of the bed.

Carter hummed low in his throat. "I see." His hand roamed over her body, as though he was reluctant to stop touching her. "Showers are overrated." He bit her earlobe softly and she squirmed against him.

Sophia laughed. "Not this morning, I'm afraid."

He kissed her, moving his hands between her legs to stroke the still-sensitive tissues there. "Are you sure?"

"Yes," she said, her voice wavering as her resolve weakened.

Carter made a humming sound low in his throat,

his fingers playing her body like it was his guitar. It didn't take long before she was panting against him, gripping his shoulders as her hips thrust against his hand.

He brought her down slowly, stroking, touching, caressing all the right places. When her breathing had returned to normal, he smacked her bottom lightly. "You'd better get started."

The thought of leaving him alone in bed all rumpled and smelling like sex was deeply unappealing. "Want to join me?" If she could convince him to come along, it would be easier to go.

Amusement flashed in his eyes. "If I get in there with you, I can promise you won't be getting clean."

The wicked promise in his voice nearly did her in. Carter grinned, apparently well aware of the effect he had on her. "Go," he said, pulling the sheets over his magnificent body as though to remove temptation.

"Fine," she grumbled, knowing he was right. She scanned the floor for her panties, but decided not to worry about it. Let him see what he was missing by not joining her in the bathroom.

She made it to the door when he said her name. She turned to find him sitting up in bed, the sheets pooled in his lap.

He met her gaze, his green eyes soft. "I just want you to know… I wasn't sleeping."

His words went straight to her heart, feeding the hope that had sprouted there since the moment she'd opened the door to find him standing on the porch with a pizza box in hand.

A smile spread across her face. "I wasn't, either."

Carter couldn't stop grinning as he drove back to Sophia's house, Margot in the seat beside him.

This morning had been perfect. There was no other word to describe it.

He still wasn't sure what had made him reach for her in the early dawn light. It had started as a reflex, something he'd done while still bogged down in sleep, his conscious mind unaware of what his body was doing. But as soon as he'd pulled Sophia against him and felt her warmth against his skin, he'd snapped awake. From that point on, he'd simply acted on instinct, driven by need, and had raced to stay ahead of his brain so that logic couldn't put the brakes on the moment.

Fortunately, she'd felt the same. But somewhere along the way, he'd let his emotions get involved. He'd stopped having sex with Sophia and instead had made love to her. He'd opened his heart, hoping she would treat it with care.

And she had. Her face had lit up when he'd told her he hadn't been sleeping, and her whispered confession had let him know she felt the same way. Even now, the memory of it electrified him from the inside out.

The rest of the morning had been idyllic. After she'd showered, he'd done the same. By the time he'd dressed, Ben had woken up and he'd fed the baby breakfast. It was an ordinary activity, the type of thing fathers did with their children every day. But for Carter, the experience had been surreal. He'd marveled at the boy's interest in eating, cheering him on as he gripped a spoon with more enthusiasm than skill. It was fascinating to watch the little one learn; during Carter's recovery, he'd had firsthand experience trying to master skills he'd once taken for granted. He loved watching Ben, the trial and error at play as the baby fed himself.

Spending the morning with Sophia and Ben had given him something to strive for. This was the kind of life he wanted for his son. Parents who loved him and each other, and a house full of laughter. He knew Sophia wanted the same thing—he'd seen the desire in her eyes when he'd caught her watching the two of them. They still had a lot to talk about, but he was confident they were on the same page and could work together to find a way forward.

He hadn't wanted to leave, hadn't wanted to break the spell. But Margot had been worried about him, and with good cause. He hadn't told her he was leaving last night. Not surprisingly, she'd been alarmed to find the apartment empty this morning. So he'd kissed both Sophia and Ben goodbye, with a promise to return soon.

Now excitement bubbled in his stomach as they drew closer to the house. Margot didn't know where they were going. He'd told her there was someone he wanted her to meet, but he hadn't gone into details. She'd smiled knowingly, though, probably thinking he was going to introduce her to a girlfriend. It would certainly explain his recent absence, but that wasn't the whole story.

She was going to love Ben—he just knew it. How could she not? He was an adorable baby, with those big green eyes and his ready smile. Even if Carter hadn't been the child's father, he would have thought he was cute.

He wished there was some way to prepare Margot for the news, but driving and signing didn't exactly mix. So he waited until he parked in front of Sophia's house and then turned to his sister.

Sophia is not just a girlfriend, he signed. *I knew her before my accident.*

Margot nodded, her hands busy. *I thought as much*, she replied. *It seemed like things were moving awfully fast for someone you'd just met.*

Carter smiled. *She's in town because of this house. She inherited it from a former customer at the bar. It's full of all his things, so she's trying to organize everything and sell the place.*

Wow, she signed. Margot turned to glance at the house. *That's quite a gift.*

Carter took a deep breath. *There's more.*

Margot waited patiently for him to gather his thoughts. Although he was her older brother, there were times when she seemed to be the wiser one. While he knew she'd love Ben, part of him was afraid of disappointing his sister. What would she think about him only now meeting his son? Yes, there had been extenuating circumstances, but would she be upset with Sophia for keeping Ben a secret for so long?

Only one way to find out.

I have a son. There. No ambiguity in that statement. *His name is Ben.*

Margot stared at him for a moment, as though she couldn't quite understand what he was trying to tell her. *A son?* she repeated, emphasizing the sign as though perhaps he'd made a mistake and had meant something else.

Carter nodded. *His name is Ben. Sophia is his mother.*

Oh. She sat with the news for a moment, processing it. When she looked at him again, he told her the rest of it.

Ben is deaf.

Deaf? Margot signed.

He nodded again. Tears filled her eyes and she reached for his hand. *I'm sorry.*

Don't be, he signed. *I'm not. He's perfect. Just like you are.*

She laughed at that and gave his hand a squeeze before releasing it. *I'm going to remind you of that the next time we get into a disagreement.*

Carter grinned, happy to see her sense of humor shining through the shock. *I wanted you to meet Sophia and Ben. She's never spent any time with someone who is deaf before. I want her to see that Ben will be just fine. And it's important for Ben to be around as much sign language as possible.* Language deprivation was a serious problem for Deaf children; those born to hearing parents often experienced delays in learning to sign and read due to their parents not knowing enough ASL to effectively teach and communicate with their children. Carter knew Sophia would never intentionally impact Ben's development in that way, but the more the little one was exposed to fluent users of ASL, the better it would be for him in the long run. Cochlear implant or not, he needed to learn sign language to move through the Deaf community.

Margot nodded. *Does he have an implant?*

Not yet, he signed. *Sophia wants him to get one, but I'm hoping to convince her otherwise. I think seeing how well you do without one will help strengthen my case.*

I'm not going to tell her how to raise her son, Margot signed.

Carter smiled, appreciating his sister's attitude. *I'm not asking you to*, he replied. *I know she has some questions about cochlear implants, and I think you're a good person to answer them. You can tell her why you don't have one, and what you know from your friends who do have them.*

All right, she replied. *But please don't put me in the middle. You two need to work this out on your own. I don't want her to resent me later.*

She won't, Carter assured her. *Are you ready to meet them?*

Margot flipped down the sun visor and took a look in the mirror. She smoothed a hand over her hair, then nodded and signed, *Yes*.

As they walked up the path to the front door, she asked, *Have you told Mom and Dad yet?*

No. He wanted to see how the meeting with Margot went first. At some point, he'd share the news with his parents. But as soon as they knew he had a son, they'd race to Alpine to meet him. Carter needed a little time to sort things out with Sophia before exposing her to the rest of his family. Her dad hadn't been around growing up, and her mom had died years ago. It sounded like her aunts meant well, but weren't that involved in her life. Meeting Carter's parents would be a shock to her system—they were loud, in-your-face huggers who entered a room with all the subtlety of a hurricane. He'd need to prepare her for that level of energy, or she might take Ben and run far, far away.

Mom's gonna lose it, Margot signed, confirming what Carter already knew. It had been hard enough getting her to leave after the accident. It was only because he hadn't had any additional surgeries scheduled, and Margot's presence by his side, that she'd been convinced to go back home and make sure Carter's dad was okay. The old man had a heart condition, which meant he shouldn't exert himself, but his father treated the doctor's orders more like guidelines than gospel truth. If his mother hadn't been there to keep his dad in check, the man would still be out mowing the lawn in the middle of summer.

I know, he replied. *I need to warn Sophia before I bring them in. Her family isn't like ours. I'll have to prepare her first.*

Good luck, Margot signed, one eyebrow raised in a knowing look.

Thanks, Carter responded, his facial expression making it clear he was being sarcastic.

He reached out to press the doorbell, excitement thrumming through him. He was eager to see the two of them again and glad to be introducing his sister to his son. While he was comfortable with sign language, it would be good for Ben to be around someone else who was deaf. Margot would be able to relate to him on a level Carter and Sophia never could. And while that knowledge sent a pang through his heart, he was glad his sister would be a part of Ben's life. Hopefully the two of them would form a strong bond that would last through the years.

A minute passed, then two. Carter frowned and pressed the doorbell again. Sophia had known he was coming right back. He knew she hadn't gone anywhere. Maybe she was dealing with a diaper change or was in the bathroom.

He gave her another minute, then tried to call. What was keeping her?

When she didn't answer, alarm spiked in his chest. He tried the doorknob, and it turned easily in his hand.

Strange. He'd heard her lock the door behind him. After last night's scare, they weren't taking any chances. The locksmith was coming in an hour to change the locks, but what if that was too late?

Heart in his throat, Carter opened the door. *Stay here*, he told his sister. If the intruder was still inside, he didn't want to put Margot in any danger.

He found her in the kitchen, lying on the floor. "Sophia!" He fell to his knees next to her, noting with horror the large lump on the side of her head and the thin trickle of blood on her cheek.

She moaned, wincing as he pulled her into his lap. "Wake up," he commanded. "You've got to wake up for me."

"Ben," she said, her voice weak and broken.

A cold chill spread through Carter's body as he got to his feet. He hated to leave her alone, but now that he knew she was still alive, he had to find the baby. He tore through the house, searching every room. *Please, be in the crib*, he pleaded silently with the universe.

But the bedroom and the crib were empty.

No! He refused to believe the baby was gone. He searched the house again, desperate for a sign of the boy. All to no avail.

He returned to the kitchen, skidding to a stop when he found Margot next to Sophia, helping her sit up. Sophia pressed a hand to her head, wincing as she looked up at him.

"Ben? Where is he?" There was a frantic edge to her voice that mirrored his emotions.

Carter shook his head, unable to form the words. Finally, he spoke around the lump in his throat. "He's gone."

Sophia let out an inhuman wail and staggered to her feet. She lurched forward, clearly intent on searching for her son.

Carter caught her before she fell, pulling her close. She struggled against him, but he held her tight. After a moment, she went limp. He carefully lowered her to the floor, then used one hand to dial 911.

"He can't be gone," she mumbled, over and over again, as though speaking the words would somehow change reality.

"We'll find him," Carter said. But fear gripped his heart so hard he thought it might shatter. Who was he trying to convince? Himself or Sophia?

"My baby is gone." She sounded numb, and he realized she was going into shock.

"We'll find him," Carter repeated, louder this time.

He just hoped it was the truth.

Chapter 12

"I am not going to the hospital." Sophia held the ice pack to her head, waving away the attentions of the EMT.

"Ma'am," the woman said again. "That cut on your temple could use some stitches. And since you were unconscious, you need to be examined by a doctor and evaluated for a head injury."

"I don't care," Sophia said. "My baby is missing. I'm not going anywhere until we find him."

The EMT shot Carter an exasperated look, but he merely shook his head.

"Fine," the woman finally said. "I can't force you to do anything. But please consider seeing a doctor soon."

Sophia looked down, feeling a little bad for giving

the EMT a hard time. She was only trying to help— it wasn't her fault Ben had been taken. "Thank you."

The woman finished packing up her bag and paused. "I'm sorry your baby was taken. I hope you find him soon."

Sophia's eyes filled with tears. She'd lost count of the number of times that had happened since she'd woken on the kitchen floor to find Carter standing over her, confirming her worst fears had come true.

"Ma'am, can you walk me through it again?" asked one of the officers.

She turned to look at him, squinting to bring him into focus. Her vision was a little blurry; perhaps the EMT was right.

But going to the hospital would take time. The police would have to follow her there to finish questioning her, and that would delay their search for Ben. She couldn't stand the thought of him with Jake, couldn't bear to imagine the ways that man could hurt her baby. If she went to the hospital and Jake harmed him, she'd never forgive herself.

So she took a deep breath and started telling her story again. The repetition was frustrating, but she knew the police were trying to do their jobs. The first set of detectives had listened to her and taken off, presumably leaving so they could start searching for Ben. A second set of officers was with her now, the same men who had responded to the break-in the previous night.

The one who had played with Ben sat to her side, studying her with a concerned look on his face. Maybe she was projecting, but he seemed a little shaken by the news that the baby he'd held not long ago was now missing.

"It was Jake," she said, gripping Carter's hand as she spoke. He hadn't left her side since she'd woken up. They'd taken turns leaning on each other, literally holding each other up in some moments. He hadn't said much, but she could tell from the tortured look in his eyes and the set of his jaw that he was just as distraught as she was.

"Carter left to go pick up his sister." She glanced at Margot, who was sitting at the far end of the table, frowning as she focused on everyone's lips. It was clear she was trying to understand, and Sophia squeezed Carter's hand. "Tell her," she said, nodding at Margot.

Carter glanced down the table and jerked a bit, as if surprised to find his sister there. Then he slid his hand free from hers and began to sign.

"And Carter is…?" the detective asked, letting the question trail off.

"Ben's father," she said. "I called him and asked him to stay with me after the break-in. He'd gone home to get his sister, because we wanted her to meet Ben. I locked the door after he left—we'd already called the locksmith, but he wasn't going to be here until later."

"Okay," the officer said. "What happened then?"

She swallowed, a chill skittering down her spine at the memory. "I heard a key in the lock. At first, I thought it was just Carter returning, but then I remembered he doesn't have a key."

"Who entered the house?"

"Jake Porter. If that's really his name."

The officer scribbled furiously in his little book. "Just to confirm, is this the same man you believe broke in last night?"

Sophia nodded, her stomach twisting as a fresh spasm of fear gripped her. "Yes."

"All right," he said. "What happened next?"

"When I realized someone was coming into the house, I grabbed Ben and rushed to the back door. I was hoping to get out that way, before he could see us."

"Smart move," muttered the officer sitting next to her.

She gave him a lopsided smile. "It would have been, but I couldn't get the door open." She glanced at Carter, knowing this next part would upset him. "We put a chair under the handle last night, to jam the door shut in case someone tried to get in that way. I couldn't pull it free and keep hold of Ben."

Carter's shoulders stiffened and he looked at her, guilt written across his face. "Soph, I'm so sorry. I should have—"

"It's not your fault," she said, cutting him off. "We had no way of knowing he'd come back, especially in broad daylight."

She turned back to the officer. "He found me there, fumbling with the chair. At first, I thought he'd leave us alone. He started yelling at me, demanding 'Where's the safe? What did you do with it?' I told him I didn't know what he was talking about. That only seemed to make him angrier."

"Is that when he hit you?" The officer gestured to her face with his pen.

Sophia shook her head and immediately wished she hadn't as the world spun around her. She closed her eyes and put her hands to her forehead. "No," she answered, swallowing hard as bile rose in her throat. "Ben started to cry. Jake stared at him for a second, and then he got this funny look on his face, like he was sad or something."

"Sad?" Carter asked, frowning.

"Yeah," she confirmed. "It freaked me out, especially because he said, 'You made me do this.' But before I could react, he grabbed hold of Ben and yanked him out of my arms." She could still feel his little body slip from her grasp, recalled that instant of panic when she'd realized she no longer had him.

"I lunged for Ben, trying to get him back. He broke away from me and ran. I chased him into the kitchen, and that's when he turned and hit me."

The blow had been unexpected, so she hadn't been able to defend herself. She'd been so intent on getting Ben back, she hadn't thought to throw up an arm when Jake had whirled suddenly. He'd grabbed a mug from the counter and clocked her with it, and her last memory was an explosion of pain and a cold sensation on her cheek that she now realized had been the linoleum of the floor. "I don't know what happened after that. I woke up to find Margot kneeling next to me, and Carter standing in the doorway."

"Do you have any idea where Jake might have taken your baby?"

"No." Frustration crept into her voice. It was the same question the detectives had asked her earlier, as though she might have special insight as to where they might be. "I don't know him at all. I have no idea who his friends are or where he hides out when he's not breaking into my house. And I don't know about this safe he wants from me." She started shaking, reality hitting her all over again.

How was she going to get her son back? She didn't know where the safe was, and without it, she didn't know how to bargain with him. There was no way he would simply hand over Ben, not after he'd gone to the trouble of kidnapping him. No, the only way she'd ever see that sweet face again, hear that delightful belly laugh and enjoy those sloppy kisses was if she gave Jake what he wanted in exchange.

If only she knew where it was!

She hadn't seen a safe or anything resembling one while going through the house. But Jake was clearly convinced one was in here, somewhere. He'd already gone through the kitchen, the living room and the china hutch in the dining room. The only places left were the bedroom and the study.

Sophia shot to her feet and headed down the hall, determined to find the safe. If she had to tear down the walls, she'd do it without hesitation if it meant getting Ben back safely.

"Ma'am? What are you doing?" the officer called

after her. But she ignored him, intent on finding what she needed.

Carter was hot on her heels, stepping into the bedroom only seconds after her. "You think it's in here?"

She shrugged, grateful she didn't have to take time to explain things to him. "I'm not sure. It's got to be here or in the study."

"I'll have Margot look there," he said. He left the room and returned a few seconds later. "Okay, she's searching there. Why don't I tackle the closet while you look through the dresser drawers and under the bed?"

Sophia nodded, already dropping to her knees. She heard footsteps in the hall and looked up to find the officer standing in the doorway. "Ma'am, we're going to leave now and issue an Amber Alert for your son. A detective will be here soon, just in case the kidnapper tries to make contact with you. In the meantime, please call if you have any new information that might help."

Sophia waved him away. "Of course. Thank you." She was too focused on the task at hand to pay him much attention. In a way, this search was a gift—if she didn't have something to do, she'd go mad with worry. Focusing on this hunt for the mysterious safe kept her from imagining any number of horrifying outcomes involving Ben and Jake, and the things he might be driven to do to her innocent baby.

There was nothing under the bed, aside from a few shoeboxes full of old family photos. The dresser drawers held clothes, a watch and a few old nightgowns that must have belonged to Will's wife. But no safe. It was the same for the bedside table. And there were no valuables, either, nothing that might have been kept in a safe at one time that she could give Jake in exchange for Ben.

Despair began to grow in her chest as her search failed to uncover the safe. Carter emerged from the closet, dust in his hair and on his clothes. She opened her mouth to ask, but based on his expression, she knew he hadn't found anything, either.

She broke down then, sobs shaking her body as she lost her grip on control. Carter gathered her close, lending her his strength.

"It's okay," he said softly. "There are other places we can look."

"Where?" she cried into his shirt. If Margot had found something, she would have already come running to tell them. The study wasn't that big—she'd likely already searched the obvious places.

Carter was quiet a moment. "There's the attic," he suggested. "Or the garage. Maybe Will was paranoid, and he buried it under some floorboards?"

She sniffed, trying not to lose hope. "Maybe," she said. Though it wasn't very likely he'd gone to the trouble of carving out a space under the floors. Still, the attic and garage were possible options.

"All right," she said, drawing a deep breath. "Let's keep moving. If we don't find a safe in the next fifteen minutes, I'm going to start ripping out drywall."

Carter offered her a smile that was part pride, part

sadness. "It won't come to that," he vowed. "We're going to find it, and we're going to get our boy back."

"I hope you're right," she whispered, hardly daring to give voice to any hint of doubt, lest the universe hear and punish her for it.

"I am," Carter insisted vehemently. "He's coming home, Soph."

She nodded, wishing she had his confidence. His willpower had carried him through the accident and his recovery, and now he was putting it to good use again. Only this time, the outcome wasn't dependent on how badly he wanted something to happen.

Their baby was in the clutches of an angry, volatile man, one who had gone from threats to break-ins to kidnapping. It didn't take an expert criminal profiler to see Jake was escalating.

And there was only one place left for him to go.

It was quiet in the truck.

Finally.

In the hour or so since he'd taken the baby, the boy hadn't stopped crying. Jake had tried distracting him with music, with videos on his phone, with anything he could think of. But the kid had just kept wailing, his eyes wide with terror and his little chest heaving like a set of bellows.

It was enough to drive him mad.

Fortunately, the baby had fallen asleep a few minutes ago. He'd cried himself into exhaustion, and while Jake felt sorry for the little guy, he was glad the assault on his ears had ended. Even though it was quiet now, the echoes of the baby's cries still hung in the air, and Jake's nerves felt raw and exposed.

He couldn't do this much longer. He'd planned on keeping the baby for several hours, enough time to get the woman all spun up and start the wheels turning. She'd call the cops, they'd come take a report, and hopefully she'd be so worried about her son she'd search the house and find the safe. Then, after he turned over the baby to the hospital, he'd waltz into the house and take it while everyone was out for the big reunion.

Of course, he hadn't planned on the boy acting so traumatized.

It wasn't like he'd hurt the kid—he wasn't a monster. But the baby screamed and cried like he was being flayed alive. It was enough to break Jake's cynical heart.

And cause him the mother of all headaches.

So as much as he'd prefer to wait a little longer, it was clear he was going to have to drop off the kid earlier than planned. He didn't know how long the baby would sleep, and he couldn't handle a second round of hysterical crying.

The boy was lying on the seat next to him, curled up in a little ball. Jake placed his hand on the baby's back, keeping him in place as he drove. Fortunately, the truck sat up higher than most of the vehicles around him, so he didn't have to worry that some nosy driver would see the little one and call the cops.

He drove carefully, trying not to jostle the kid too much. He pulled into the staff parking lot of the hospital, donned a baseball cap and pulled the brim down low.

It only took a few minutes. He spied a woman walking through the lot, headed to her car. She held a mug in one hand and had her purse and a lunch bag strung over her shoulder. Her blue scrubs were a little wrinkled, as though she'd been wearing them awhile.

She'd do.

Jake quickly hopped out of the truck and circled around to the passenger side. He picked up the baby, who let out a small whine of protest but didn't fully awaken.

Walking fast, he approached the woman. "Excuse me, do you work here?"

She drew up short, eyes scanning him and the baby. "Yeah. The emergency room is right there." She pointed to the clearly marked entrance to the left, obviously thinking he was here to have the baby seen.

He shook his head. "That's okay." He stepped close, and before she could protest, he pressed the baby to her. She grabbed him instinctively, and Jake turned and jogged back to the car.

"Hey!" she yelled. "What the hell are you doing?"

"Call the police," he hollered over his shoulder. "They'll know who he is."

He heard the familiar wail of the baby start up again and slammed the door of his truck, dulling the sound. Then he cranked the engine and punched the gas, tearing out of the lot before the woman could come after him.

He glanced in the rearview mirror as he drove

away, wanting to make sure the woman wasn't going to hurt the kid. All he could see was her back as she headed into the hospital.

"Good," he muttered. They'd know how to take care of him while they waited for the police to arrive. The little one would be back with his mother in no time. He felt bad about traumatizing the kid, but there'd been no other way. He had to get that money and get out of town before Richard's men started sniffing around.

He headed back to his grandfather's neighborhood, careful to obey all the traffic laws as he drove. He couldn't get pulled over now, not when he was so close to finally getting what he needed.

The tree-lined street was quiet. He saw that man's truck parked in the driveway, and a dark sedan at the curb. *Detectives*, he thought. But the scene was quieter than he'd anticipated. Good. Maybe she was already searching for the safe.

Jake cracked the windows and hunkered down in his seat, settling in to watch the house. It shouldn't take long for word to spread that the kidnapped baby had turned up at the hospital. He glanced at his watch. Fifteen, maybe thirty minutes before she got the news? Once that happened, he figured she and everyone else would rush to the hospital, leaving the house empty.

And that was when he'd make his move.

Chapter 13

Carter paced the living room, unable to stay still. A dull ache in his hips accompanied his every step, but he ignored it. He had to keep moving, to fight that creeping sense of powerlessness that was threatening to take over. If he sat, he'd surrender to despair and hopelessness. They were familiar emotions, ones he'd flirted with a lot in the immediate aftermath of his accident. He'd clawed his way free once, but it had taken all his willpower and energy. If those terrible feelings got hold of him a second time, he wasn't sure he'd be able to escape again.

All his thoughts were focused on Ben. Where was he? Was he okay? Was Jake being kind to him, or was he hurting the baby? His hands clenched into fists at the thought of harm coming to his son.

The police had to find him. They simply had to. He refused to even think about the alternative.

He glanced at Sophia. She was sitting on the sofa looking completely shell-shocked, her eyes staring into the distance but not really seeing anything. A detective sat nearby, trying to talk to her. It was clear the man was trying to help, but Sophia would only nod or shake her head in response to his statements.

Their search of the house had proved fruitless. Margot hadn't found anything in the study, and the bedroom and closet had been empty, as well. The safe wasn't in the garage or the attic, either. Either Jake was mistaken, or Will had hidden it so well they would never find it.

Sophia had crumpled when they'd finished looking, folding in on herself like a deflated balloon. She'd been running on fierce determination and a mother's hope, and now that hope was gone. Carter had held her for as long as she'd let him, trying to give her strength. She had to keep going, had to believe Ben would be okay. But she'd dropped onto the couch and retreated into her mind, pulling further inward with every passing second.

It was terrifying to watch, but Carter didn't know what to do to bring her back. If this went on for much longer, he was afraid he was going to lose her forever. She was hollowing out before his eyes, becoming a shell of herself. If something good didn't happen, and soon, she'd never recover.

He began to wander through the house, drifting from room to room aimlessly. He wound up in the bathroom, splashed some water on his face. It didn't help. He put his palms on the counter and leaned forward, head down until it was almost touching the mirror. Emotions swirled and built in his chest, anger bubbling to the surface. His son was missing. The woman he cared about was falling apart in the next room. And what was he doing about it? Nothing.

He glanced up, staring at his reflection. A muscle in his jaw twitched, and his green eyes blazed. Before he could think twice, Carter drew back his arm and punched the mirror.

Pain exploded in his fist and ricocheted up his arm. He welcomed the sensation, the distraction that it brought. His reflection splintered into a thousand different facets, thanks to the starburst cracks his fist had left in the glass. Good. He didn't have to look at himself any longer, see the failure he was.

He dropped his head again, breathing hard. His anger ebbed away, replaced by the insistent throb of his hand. He flexed his fingers, noting with dispassion that he was bleeding. A line of cuts crisscrossed his knuckles, and tiny shards of glass winked in the light. Feeling foolish now, he ran his hand under the water and wrapped it in a towel. Then he knelt and opened the cabinet under the sink, hoping to find some bandages.

There were rolls of toilet paper, some cotton swabs. And a small black case tucked in the back, flush against the wall. Carter's breath caught in his throat. Was that—? Could it really be—?

He reached into the depths of the cabinet, his hand

shaking and his heart in his throat. The case was bulky, made of a thick, textured plastic. It took two hands to pull it free, and once he got it into the light, he saw a handle tucked against the side, along with a lock set flush with the plastic.

The safe.

He hugged it to his chest and ran for the living room. "I've got it!" he yelled, unable to contain his excitement.

The detective looked up in alarm when he entered the room, and even Margot jumped at the sight of him. But Sophia didn't react. Carter ran to her and knelt, taking her hands in one of his. "Sophia, I found the safe."

Her eyes flicked to him then, a spark of curiosity flaring in the brown depths. "What?" she whispered. Her voice sounded cracked, as though it had broken along with her heart.

Carter placed the lockbox in her lap, relieved to see the life come back into her face as she registered what she was holding.

"Oh, my God," she said softly. Tears filled her eyes and she looked at him, her lower lip trembling. "You found it."

Carter nodded, reaching up to brush her hair behind her ear. He laughed, feeling positively giddy. "It was in the bathroom, under the sink," he said. "Who puts a safe in the bathroom?"

Dimly, he heard a phone ring from somewhere in the room, then the soft voice of the detective as he answered the call. "We've got it," he said to Sophia. "We can get our boy back."

She nodded, gripping him with one hand and the box with the other. "What—what happened to your hand?"

He glanced down, noted the towel wrapped around his fist. "Nothing," he said, shaking his head. "That's nothing."

Sophia lifted one eyebrow, conveying her skepticism. But she didn't press the issue. "How do we get in touch with Jake? We have to let him know we have the safe." She glanced at the detective, who had retreated to the corner to finish his call. "There has to be some way we can reach him."

"I don't know," Carter said. In the movies, there was always a number the kidnapper called to demand his ransom. But Jake didn't have their phone numbers, so how would he be able to contact them? "Maybe he can call the police, and they'll patch him through to us?" But that sounded far-fetched. His earlier elation began to fade as he realized that although they had found the safe, they weren't any closer to getting Ben back.

Sophia bit her bottom lip, her expression thoughtful. "What about the news? We could have them announce we found the safe and want to trade. If he's watching, he'll know to get in touch."

"It's worth a shot," Carter agreed. Anything to get their son back.

The detective walked over, grinning from ear to ear. "I've got good news, people. Your baby was dropped off at the hospital about twenty minutes ago. He's waiting for you now."

Sophia sat in the back of the detective's car, practically vibrating off the seat. It was a good thing the detective had offered to drive, because there was no way she could have handled that right now. He stopped at a red light, and it took all her willpower not to jump out of the car and start running.

Carter's hand on her arm distracted her. She turned to look at him and saw understanding in his eyes. "I know," he said softly. "Almost there."

He was just as excited, leaning forward as though that might force the car to go faster. Margot sat in the front seat, twisting her hair in a gesture that betrayed her nerves. Now that she knew her baby was safe, Sophia felt her heart go out to the other woman. It had to be difficult, thinking you were coming to meet your nephew only to find him gone, unable to do more than watch helplessly as your brother and his girlfriend fell to pieces in front of your eyes.

She'd been a source of quiet strength, and Sophia was glad Margot had been there through it all. She'd seen the way Carter had looked at his sister during that seemingly endless stretch of time when her hope of ever seeing Ben again had waned. Carter had drawn comfort from Margot's presence, and Sophia was immensely grateful. She'd been so wrapped up in her own head and overcome by fear that she hadn't been able to help Carter. He'd done his best to support her, but she'd been beyond help. At least he'd had someone there for him.

The safe bumped against the door as the detective turned. He'd asked Carter to bring it to the hospital, saying one of the officers there could pick the lock. Sophia didn't care about its contents—she just wanted to see her baby again. She knew Carter felt the same way, but he'd done as the man asked and carried it out to the car when they'd left.

After what seemed like an eternity, the detective parked the car. Without waiting for him to cut the engine, Sophia jumped out and headed for the hospital entrance at a run. She heard the detective's voice behind her, trying to tell her something, but she couldn't wait. She had to get to Ben.

She ran through the automatic doors and skidded to a stop at the information desk. An older woman wearing a pin that read Ask Me! I'm a Volunteer! on the front of her shirt leaned back in alarm. "Can I—?" she began.

"My baby," Sophia said, a little breathless. "I'm here for my son. He was brought in half an hour ago. His name is Ben."

The woman nodded and began typing on a computer. "Last name?"

She heard the automatic doors swish behind her, and then Carter, Margot and the detective were there. "He's this way, ma'am," the detective said. He flashed his badge at the volunteer and, without breaking stride, took Sophia's arm and led her deeper into the hospital.

They bypassed the reception desk at the ER. The

nurse buzzed them through when the detective held up his badge again, and he led them past the triage room into the ER bay. Three beds were lined up along each wall, rows of curtains hanging from the ceiling for the sake of privacy. Sophia scanned the place, searching desperately for her son. All the bays were empty. Where was he?

"In here," the detective said kindly. There was a door just past the nurses' station. He opened it, and she saw her baby inside.

Relief made her stagger. Carter wrapped his arm around her and half dragged, half carried her into the room.

Ben was sitting on a gurney, gripping a stuffed animal as a nurse fed him applesauce with a plastic spoon. Two other nurses were there, cooing and smiling at him. A uniformed officer stood in the corner, looking on with a smile. For his part, Ben seemed fine. She didn't see any bruises, scrapes or cuts. He was eating applesauce like a champ, as though this was the most normal thing in the world. But for a moment, Sophia couldn't breathe.

Ben turned to look at her, and as soon as their eyes met, he burst into tears. He threw the stuffed animal to the floor and lunged for her. She scooped him into her arms and gripped him tight, pressing him against her chest and banding her arms around his precious little body. She buried her nose in the fold of his neck and inhaled, drawing that sweet baby scent deep into her lungs.

He burrowed against her, fists gripping her shirt

as though he was afraid she'd let him go. Like there was any chance of that.

She wasn't sure how long they stood there. She heard a sniffle and opened her eyes to find everyone watching her.

One of the nurses swiped tears from her eyes. "Sweet boy," she said, patting Ben's back as she walked past. "You're all right now."

The women filed out of the room one by one while Sophia held Ben. She thanked them, tears welling up. She felt at a loss—how did she thank them for taking care of her son the way they had? But she tried her best.

"He's okay, Mama," said the last nurse just before she left the room. "The doctor will be in soon to give you all the details, but he's fine."

The last of Sophia's worry melted away in the face of that reassurance. The uniformed officer and the detective left the room, too.

"We'll give you all a minute," the detective said as he stepped into the hall.

Sophia turned to face Carter, unable to contain her smile. "He's here," she said.

Carter nodded, tears streaming down his face. "And he's perfect."

He placed his hand on Ben's back. Their son turned to look at him, and joy bloomed in Sophia's heart when she saw the brilliant smile light up Ben's face.

"Hey, little man," Carter both said and signed. "You doing okay?"

Ben began to move his hands, clearly trying to

communicate. Carter and Sophia both laughed at his enthusiasm. "He seems okay now."

They sat on the bed together, Ben between them. Sophia was so absorbed in her son that she'd forgotten Margot was still in the room. It wasn't until the other woman sat in the chair in the corner that she tuned back in.

"Oh!" she said, meeting Margot's eyes. *I'm sorry,* she signed. *I was too—* She tried to make the sign for *overwhelmed,* but based on Margot's small smile, she probably missed the mark.

Margot shook her head, waving off the apology. *It's okay,* she signed slowly and carefully. *Don't worry about it.*

Carter stepped in. *Come meet Ben,* he signed.

Her eyes lit up and she moved forward, pulling the chair closer.

Ben studied her as she drew near, leaning against Carter's side and half hiding his face. Margot didn't press the issue. She leaned back in the chair and began signing, her hands moving slowly so Ben could follow the movements.

After a few seconds, he grinned at her. She made the sign for *aunt* several times, and Sophia smiled as he mimicked her. Margot clapped, then pointed at Carter and made the sign for *daddy.* Once again, Ben copied her, bouncing with excitement at Margot's obvious delight.

Sophia watched them communicate, her heart soaring as she saw the way Ben responded to his aunt. He was clearly thrilled to be signing, and Margot was a patient teacher, just like her brother. As she studied the three of them—Ben, his father and Margot—she realized she couldn't take him back to El Paso. She was trying her best to learn sign language, but Carter and Margot were fluent. Ben needed that kind of contact, that regular exposure to effortless communication that she couldn't give him. It broke her heart a little to know she couldn't be everything her son needed, but she couldn't let her ego get in the way of his development. She owed it to him to give him the best start in life. If that meant staying in Alpine so he could be with his father and his aunt, then so be it.

And as for graduate school? Perhaps she could find a way to complete her research off-site. She'd already finished her coursework. Lots of students went elsewhere for the research part of their degree—many traveled to places like Hawaii, or other sites with large telescopes. With Big Bend being so remote, she could probably do some of her studies in the park. Hopefully her adviser would understand. And if she didn't? Well, Ben was more important than a degree.

The only uncertainty left to work out was Carter. He'd probably be thrilled to have her and Ben stay in town—she knew he already loved the boy to distraction. But what about their relationship? Should they try to give it a go, or should they put their focus solely on Ben?

Her mind drifted back to the morning. It felt like a lifetime ago, though it hadn't been that long since they'd slept together. They'd both agreed to shut off their brains and just feel, but she'd still been intending to go back to El Paso then. It was one thing to give in to attraction knowing their time together had a natural end point. But now that she knew she was planning to stay, would Carter be happy to be around her, or would it make things awkward between them?

It doesn't matter, she told herself. She was doing this for Ben, because he needed his father. Not because she wanted a lover.

Or was she just lying to herself?

Carter glanced up, catching her eye. He shot her a questioning look. Sophia shook her head. "Later," she said softly. Once they were home, with this nightmare behind them, they could talk.

There was a loud rap on the door, and it opened to reveal a barrel-chested man in a white coat. "Hello," he said, voice booming in the small room. "I'm Dr. Bradford. I'm the pediatrician who examined Ben."

Sophia introduced herself, and Carter shook hands with the man and introduced his sister. "Is everything okay?" he asked. Even though the nurse had told her Ben was fine, she still felt a tremor of worry. What if a test had come back with bad news?

"He's fine," the man said, smiling at them. "I saw no bumps or bruises, no signs of any kind of abuse."

Sophia exhaled and relief flashed across Carter's face, as well. "That's good," he said, running his hand over the top of Ben's head.

Dr. Bradford frowned a little. "There was something I wanted to talk to you about, though."

Sophia's heart skipped a beat. "What? What is it?"

The doctor lifted one shoulder. "Ben doesn't respond to his name. Doesn't respond to any sounds at all, actually. He makes eye contact appropriately, and shows interest in faces, so I don't think he has a neurodevelopmental issue. I don't want to scare you all, but have you had his hearing evaluated?"

Sophia let out a short laugh, startling the man. "He's deaf," she explained.

The doctor nodded, understanding dawning on his face. "Well, that definitely explains it," he said. "Ben's discharge paperwork is processing now. It should be ready in a few minutes. Do you have any questions for me?"

Sophia shook her head, and Carter did the same. "Thank you, Doctor," she murmured, feeling a surge of gratitude toward the large man. He clearly cared about Ben, and she appreciated the way he'd told her about his concerns.

"Anytime," Dr. Bradford replied. He turned and left the room, holding the door open so two officers and the detective could enter.

The detective carried the safe. He placed it on the small table and grinned at Ben. "I'm glad the little guy is safe."

"We are, too," Carter said. He placed his hand on the baby's side, holding him close.

Sophia looked at the officers, men she felt like she knew, thanks to their frequent visits over the last day or so. "Did you find him?"

They shook their heads. "Not yet," said the one who always took notes.

"But we will," his partner added. He waved at Ben, but the baby only had eyes for his aunt.

"We did speak to the attorney who handled Will Porter's will. He had called yesterday afternoon to report a visit from Jake that had left him uncomfortable. He said Jake Porter thinks you manipulated his grandfather into changing his will to exclude him. He's convinced if he can find the original copy of the will, he can use it to prove his grandfather was not of sound mind when he wrote the revisions."

"So that's why he's obsessed with getting the safe," Sophia said.

"Yeah," the detective confirmed. "But that's not all."

"We did some digging in to Jake Porter," the second officer told her. "Seems he's a gambler, and not a very successful one at that. He's bounced from Atlantic City to Vegas, and he recently lost his car in a game."

"No wonder he wants the will," Sophia said. "He needs his grandfather's money." There had been a tidy sum left in Will's accounts that had gone to her—not enough to make her rich, but enough that she didn't have to worry about bills for a while.

The men all nodded. "The attorney said there might be cash in the safe, as well. He didn't think Jake would have the patience to deal with a protracted legal battle, especially when he doesn't have a leg to stand on."

"Do you think someone's after him?" Sophia asked. "He seemed…desperate when he attacked me this morning. If he's hoping to prove the house should have gone to him, he's not going about it the right way."

"That's definitely possible," one of the officers replied. "He doesn't exactly keep good company. He might have run afoul of some of the other gamblers in town, maybe owes an unsavory character some money. He probably hoped to get the safe and hit the road before the law caught up to him."

Carter eyed the lockbox. "Can you open it?"

"We can try," the detective said. "The attorney said that whatever is inside is yours, Miss Burns. It's considered part of the property and assets Mr. Porter bequeathed to you."

Sophia nodded, feeling uncertain. That small plastic case had brought so much misery into her life, she was tempted to chuck it in the dumpster and walk away. But curiosity nudged at her, making her wonder what, exactly, was inside.

She had to know.

Carter filled in Margot on the conversation while one of the officers pulled a thin file from his pocket and set to work picking the lock. After a few minutes, he leaned back with a flourish. "Done!" he exclaimed, clearly pleased with himself.

Everyone turned to Sophia. "You should do the honors," Carter said. "After all, it belongs to you."

She hopped off the bed and walked to the small table, then lifted the lid.

The interior was small, not much larger than a long envelope. And at first glance, that was all that appeared to be inside.

She pulled one envelope free, peeking inside. "I think this is the will," she said, passing it to Carter.

A second envelope held a bundle of cash. Judging by the appearance of the bills, they'd been tucked away for decades.

The last item in the safe was a small velvet sack. Sophia opened it to find a diamond pendant, a gold bracelet and a diamond wedding ring set inside.

"His wife's," she said, tears pricking her eyes.

"That's got to be worth some money," the detective mused.

"And there's a little over two thousand dollars here," Carter said. "Probably enough to get Jake out of whatever trouble he's in."

"Maybe once," agreed one of the officers. "But not anymore."

The officer who was the note-taker wrote down the contents of the safe. Then he flipped his pad shut and tucked it back into his pocket. "All right, ma'am. We'll be in touch to let you know how the investigation is going. In the meantime, you're all free to go home."

"Thank you," she said. Carter stood and shook everyone's hand while she made sure Ben didn't fall off the bed. She should be happy to be leaving, but a large part of her didn't want to go back to the house. After last night's break-in and this morning's kidnapping, she didn't know if she'd ever feel safe there again.

Her emotions must have shown on her face. Margot got her attention and signed, *Are you okay?*

Sophia smiled and nodded. It was silly to be afraid of a house. And with the entire Alpine Police Department searching for Jake, it would be stupid for him to stick around. She and Ben would be fine.

Eventually.

Jake sat on the edge of the hotel bed, breathing hard. So close. He'd been so close to getting the safe.

He'd watched them bolt out of the house, presumably after getting the news about the boy. They'd all left—the woman, the man, the cop. And a second woman he hadn't seen before. The place was empty, his for the plunder.

But then he'd noticed the small black case the man was carrying.

The safe.

They'd found it.

He'd watched them pile in the car, anger building in his chest as his ticket to freedom sped away.

To make matters worse, Richard had chosen that moment to call.

Jake hadn't answered, letting it go to voice mail. That had been a mistake. He could tell as soon as he heard Richard's voice that the other man wasn't happy about being ignored.

"I tried to be nice about this," the message said. "I wanted to give you the benefit of the doubt. But I won't tolerate your disrespect."

It was clear Richard had taken the gloves off his enforcers. If they caught up to him, there was no telling what they'd do. He needed to get out of town, pronto, but he wasn't going to make it very far without the cash in that safe.

There was only one option left. He walked to his duffel and dug through it until his fingers brushed cold, smooth metal.

Jake pulled the revolver free and checked the cylinder. Everything looked good. He shoved it into the waistband of his pants and tossed his duffel over his shoulder. He wasn't coming back here. Once he got that safe, he was heading out.

He climbed behind the wheel of his rental and sighed, then ran his hand over his face. "It wasn't supposed to be like this," he muttered to himself.

But now there was no other way.

Chapter 14

Carter put the last of the books in a box and turned to Sophia with a smile. "There," he said. "It looks much better already."

She nodded. "That it does."

They'd spent the last few hours putting the rooms back to rights, erasing all signs of Jake's intrusion last night and their frantic search from this morning. Margot had played with the baby, and once Ben had gone down for his nap, she'd helped them put things away. Working together, they'd gotten everything cleaned up, leaving no evidence of trouble.

The locksmith had come and gone, installing new dead bolts and adding safety chains on all the exterior doors. Carter felt much better knowing the house was more secure, and he could tell Sophia was relieved, as well. He was still planning on having her and Ben stay with him at night, but since she was determined to get things organized during the day, he was glad she'd be safe while they worked.

They sat in the living room, sipping on water as they rested. Margot tapped on her phone, smiling as she stared at the screen.

She glanced up, caught them watching her and blushed.

Let me guess, Carter signed. *Mike?*

She nodded. *He wants to take me to an early dinner*, she replied. *Are you guys okay with me leaving?*

Of course, Carter told her.

He filled in Sophia, and she nodded. "Absolutely," she said, signing *yes* with great emphasis. *You've done so much today*, she added, her hands faltering as she tried to relay her thoughts in sign language.

Carter helped her out, though he was pleased to see she didn't stop trying just because he was supplementing her efforts.

It didn't take long for Mike to arrive. Margot hugged him and Sophia, then practically danced out the door. Carter was glad to see her happy, especially after the scary events of the day.

He and Sophia returned to their seats, and she leaned against him. He put his arm around her, enjoying the feel of her against him.

It was a nice moment, the kind of ordinary domestic event that happened millions of times a day the world over. But Carter didn't think he'd ever take these peaceful interludes for granted again.

"I've been thinking," he said huskily. He and Sophia had so much to talk about, and while it would be nice to wait for the perfect moment, he knew it would never come. Based on how quickly they'd put these rooms back together, it wasn't going to take long to go through the house and get the place ready to sell. She and Ben would be headed back to El Paso before he knew it.

She chuckled. "What a coincidence. I have been, too..."

Carter took a deep breath, preparing to bare his soul. "I know you have to go back to El Paso," he said. "What would you think if I came with you?" He'd been thinking about a lot—not necessarily moving to El Paso, but about what he was going to do for a job. Over the last several weeks, he'd come to realize he couldn't go back to being a park ranger. But with his background in biology and his love of conservation, he thought he could find work as a teacher. It would be a good job, one he could enjoy. And one he could handle, physically. Best of all, he didn't have to stay in Alpine. He could get his teaching certification and work at one of the schools in El Paso, and then Houston, after Sophia got her dream job at NASA.

He told her as much, his voice rising with excitement as he shared his thoughts. Moving to El Paso would mean he could see Ben all the time. And, hopefully, he and Sophia could build their connection, as well, becoming more than just co-parents.

Making love to her this morning had left him feeling hopeful about their future. And after losing Ben, he knew he couldn't last a day without seeing his son.

Sophia was quiet, processing his idea. Carter held his breath, waiting for her to respond.

"That's the thing," she said slowly. "I'm not sure I want to move back to El Paso."

Shock zinged through him, followed closely by confusion. "I don't understand. Don't you have to finish your studies?"

"I think I can do that off-site," she explained. "I'll have to talk to my adviser, but I won't be the first student to work outside of El Paso."

"But why would you do that?"

She pulled away, smiling up at him. "I saw you today, with Ben. You and Margot. And I watched the way he responded to you both. He needs you in his life. Not just because you're his father, but because he needs to be around people who sign as easily as they breathe. I can't give him that." A shadow crossed her face, and he squeezed her arm. "But you and Margot can. I don't want to take that away from him."

"Oh, Soph." Her devotion to Ben was absolute, her words a testament to the depth of her love for him. "I'll always be a part of his life. But Margot isn't going to stay in Alpine forever. Her life is in Austin. That's where my parents live, too."

Sophia's expression turned thoughtful. "Isn't there a large school for the Deaf there?"

Carter nodded. "That's where she went, actually."

"And I know the university has an excellent astronomy program," she said, leaning forward as she spoke. "Maybe I could collaborate with someone to complete my research?"

She sounded excited by the prospect, and Carter felt his own enthusiasm begin to build. Compared to Alpine, Austin had a lot more to offer in terms of resources for Deaf children and support for their parents. It would be a much better place for Ben, and it would be nice to be closer to his family. But he didn't want to pressure Sophia, so he didn't mention that. This was the first of many conversations—there would be time to discuss all this later.

Besides, there was something else he wanted to know.

He cleared his throat, gathering his courage. "There's something else I wanted to ask you."

She placed her head on his shoulder and laid her hand on his thigh. "Shoot."

"What about us?"

She was so still, he thought for a second she hadn't heard him. Or maybe she just didn't want to answer him.

Then she sighed. "To tell you the truth," she confessed, "I'm not sure."

He absorbed her words silently. It wasn't the response he'd been hoping for, but it wasn't a rejection, either. He felt strange, as though he was hanging between two extremes. Based on her reply, he didn't know whether to be happy or upset.

"Okay," he said slowly.

"I—I want you." She huffed out a laugh. "I think

that's pretty obvious. But I don't want to put Ben at risk of losing his father."

Carter frowned, tamping down his pleasure at her admission of attraction. "Why do you think he'd lose me?"

Sophia pulled back and looked at him like he had two heads. "If we don't work out," she said, her tone making it clear she thought this should be obvious. "I don't want Ben to grow up without a dad if you and I break up."

"You think I'd leave him if we weren't together," Carter mused. Of course she did. That was the example her own father had set, so why would she think any differently?

He turned to face her and took her hands in his. "Sophia," he said, his voice grave. "I would never walk away from Ben just because you and I aren't together."

He saw the emotions warring in her eyes. It was clear she wanted to believe him, but a flicker of doubt still remained. "But how do you know?" she whispered. "How can you be so sure?"

"I'm here now, aren't I?" he asked. "I know I just found out about Ben, but I've been here ever since. And you and I aren't even officially together."

She nodded thoughtfully. "That's true, I suppose." She looked up at him, her expression guardedly hopeful. "Do you really think we have a shot?"

"Poor choice of words," a voice said from the doorway. Sophia jumped and Carter turned to see a tall, blond-haired man standing a few feet away, pointing a gun at them.

He walked in, eyes fixed on the two of them. *Jake*, Carter realized. Who else could it be?

Anger pushed him to his feet, and he moved to stand in front of Sophia. This was the man who had taken his son, threatened his woman. And now he was here, interrupting their lives once again. "Where is Ben?"

Regret flashed across Jake's face. "He's fine. Still sleeping." He paused, lowering his hand a fraction of an inch. "I didn't hurt him," he said, craning his head to try to see past Carter. "I'm not the kind of guy who hurts kids."

Carter felt Sophia shift behind him and moved to keep his body between Jake and Sophia.

"No, you're the kind who kidnaps them and knocks their mother unconscious," Carter growled. "The kind who breaks into a house in the middle of the night and terrorizes a woman living alone."

"I didn't want to do any of that, all right?" Jake yelled. He lifted the gun and pointed it at Carter's chest. "I just want the safe. All you have to do is give it to me, and I'll leave. You'll never see me again."

"How did you even get in here?" Sophia demanded. "We changed the locks."

"You were gone a long time," Jake replied. "I snuck in while you were out. Now give me the safe."

The thought of Jake lurking somewhere in the house while they'd been working sent a chill down his spine. Sophia had put Ben down for his nap half an hour ago. Had Jake watched from the shadows while she'd rocked the baby? Had he heard her singing to the boy? Stayed hidden while the little one drifted off to sleep, thinking he was safe and protected?

"The safe!" Jake demanded, breaking into Carter's thoughts.

"We don't have it," Carter said. It was the truth. They'd removed the contents and placed everything in a drawer, then thrown the thing away. Sophia had never wanted to see it again, and Carter couldn't blame her.

"Liar!" Jake screamed. He took a step forward, arm extended. "I saw you carrying it earlier. I know you found it!"

"We did," Sophia informed him. "But we don't have it any longer."

"Where is it?" Jake's voice was frantic.

Carter realized if they didn't give him something, he was liable to shoot them all. "It's in the kitchen," he said, needing to draw Jake out of the living room, away from Sophia and as far away from Ben as possible. "Just put the gun down, and I'll show you."

"No," Jake snapped. "You'll show me now. And no tricks," he added, glaring at him. "Or I'll shoot you and then come back and kill her, too."

Carter's blood turned to ice at his words. Jake had a dangerous gleam in his eyes that convinced Carter he wasn't making an idle threat.

"No tricks," Carter said, holding up his hands, palms out, to show he wasn't going to try anything. He set off for the kitchen slowly, mind whirling. What was he going to do after drawing Jake into the other room? He could give him the contents of the safe, and hopefully he'd leave. But something told him that Jake wasn't going to be satisfied with two thousand dollars in cash and his grandmother's old jewelry. He'd want more, and he wouldn't believe Carter when he told him that was all that had been inside.

He swallowed hard, considering another option. He could go on the attack. He didn't have a weapon, but maybe he could grab something from the kitchen to use to defend himself. He didn't think this was going to end well for him, but he wasn't going to go down without a fight.

All that mattered was Sophia and Ben. Hopefully she was sneaking into the bedroom now to get their son and make a run for it.

He stepped into the kitchen, eyes scanning the counters in search of something, anything he could use as a weapon. There was a knife block next to the stove. The old saying about bringing a knife to a gunfight flitted through his mind, but what other choice did he have?

"It's over here," Carter said, walking to the stove. "We put the things in this drawer." He reached out, hoping his back would hide his actions as he wrapped his hand around the hilt of the chef's knife.

There was a solid thunk behind him, and a small cry. Carter whirled, knife in hand, to see Sophia standing behind Jake. She held an old baseball bat in her hands and was wielding it like a pro, bringing her arms up to take another swing at Jake.

The man staggered under the blow, but he didn't drop the gun. He turned to face Sophia, snarling at her as he lifted the weapon.

Carter acted without thinking. He raised his arm and brought down the knife, burying it in Jake's shoulder.

Jake howled in pain and collapsed. The gun clattered to the floor, and Sophia grabbed it.

Carter took a step back, shock coursing through him. He'd just stabbed a man. He'd never even hit anyone before, much less stabbed someone. He could still feel the vibration of it traveling up his arm, the scrape of the blade against Jake's bone.

The knife slipped out of the wound as the other man moved. It hit the floor with a clang, slick with blood.

Jake clutched his arm, cursing loudly. He dropped his head and saw the knife. Then everything seemed to happen in slow motion.

Carter stepped forward, determined to kick away the knife. Jake grabbed it, dodging his leg. Carter couldn't stop his forward motion, and he wound up in Jake's reach. Jake grinned evilly and drew his arm back, knowing he had him.

Carter tried to angle away from Jake. He raised his arm in defense, bracing for the slice of the knife.

Then a deafening boom split the air and Jake was thrown against him. They landed in a heap on the floor, Jake half on top of him and Carter's knee screaming in pain.

Carter pushed Jake off him, and the man slid

across the floor until his back hit the refrigerator. Jake didn't move—his body was limp—and Carter watched in horrified relief as a pool of blood spread out from beneath him.

Carter looked up to find Sophia standing a few feet away, still clutching the gun.

"Sophia."

She didn't respond, and he realized she probably couldn't hear him. The gunshot had left his ears ringing and had probably had the same effect on her, as well.

After a few seconds, she lowered her arms. When she looked at him, her eyes were full of tears. "What did I do?" she gasped, dropping to her knees beside him.

Carter gathered her into his arms, pressing her face into his chest so she didn't have to look at Jake's body. "You protected yourself and your son. And you saved my life."

She suddenly jerked back. "Ben!" she said, panic in her voice.

Sophia got to her feet and ran out of the room, clearly intent on checking on their son.

Carter took one last look at Jake. Satisfied he was no longer a threat, he struggled to his feet and hobbled after Sophia.

He found her in the bedroom, standing over the crib. His heart in his throat, Carter staggered over, needing to see the baby for himself.

Ben was sleeping peacefully on his stomach, his

legs curled up underneath his body and his cheek pressed against the mattress.

Relief hit him in a wave that nearly knocked him over. His breath came out in a gust, and Sophia turned to him. "He's okay," she said, tears streaming down her face.

Carter could only nod. He took a step back, wincing as pain radiated out from his knee.

It was then that Sophia noticed his troubles. She slipped his arm over her shoulders and took some of his weight. Together, they shuffled back into the living room and collapsed onto the sofa, arms wrapped around each other.

Carter pressed a kiss to the top of Sophia's head, breathing in the scent of her shampoo. Gratitude and relief filled him in equal measure. She was safe. Ben was safe. They were going to be okay.

"I love you," he blurted. "I know it's not the right time to say it, but I do. I love you, and I love Ben, and I am never letting you go again."

Sophia tightened her grip on him and pressed her cheek to his chest. "I love you, too," she said, her voice thick with emotion. "And we're not going anywhere."

Epilogue

Six months later

Carter tossed the ball into the room, sending it bouncing across the wood floor. Ben squealed and ran after it, his little legs pumping as he chased after the moving target.

Sophia smiled as she watched Ben and Carter play in the empty space. It was still hard to believe this was their home. They'd signed the final paperwork this morning, and the key was in her pocket.

It was perfect—exactly the kind of place she'd hoped to raise a family in. Quiet neighborhood street, decent-size backyard, close to the park. And it was halfway between the university and the high school where Carter's new job was located. It was like the house had been made just for them, and she couldn't wait to start arranging the furniture.

Carter caught her eye and grinned as he sent the ball bouncing again for Ben. "I think he likes it here."

"Most definitely," she said. She walked over to the window, looking out on the backyard. Wild roses grew along the fence, and the yard was big enough for a dog, if they decided to get one.

"Who am I kidding?" she muttered. Of course they were going to get one.

Ben's laughter echoed in the empty room, making her heart happy. He'd shown no lasting effects from his brief kidnapping, aside from being extra clingy in the days after the ordeal. She, on the other hand, had needed some therapy to deal with her emotions after killing Jake. Nightmares had plagued her dreams in the weeks after, but they'd gradually stopped, thanks to her therapist.

And Carter.

Every time she'd woken in the dark, a scream trapped in her throat and her body drenched in sweat, he'd been there. To hold her, to comfort her, to reassure her that Ben was safe and there was no danger.

It had taken months of work, but she no longer felt guilty about killing Jake. She wished things had turned out differently, but he had made his choices. She couldn't beat herself up for the rest of her life for defending her son and protecting the man she loved.

Therapy had helped her with other issues, as well. She was more confident in her relationship with Carter, no longer worried that if they fought or ended things he would walk out of Ben's life. Not that she had any intention of ending things with him. They'd grown closer over the last six months, their bond strengthening with every passing day. She couldn't imagine her life without him now, and didn't even want to try.

They'd come to an agreement on the cochlear implant for Ben. After lots of talking and doing more research, Sophia had agreed that it would be best to forgo the operation. They both wanted Ben to become fluent in sign language and explore Deaf culture, and if he decided to get a cochlear implant later, when he was older, they'd support him. The decision had brought no small measure of relief—Sophia had been worried about the prospect of surgery, and anxious at the thought that Ben might not be happy with the implant as he got older. This way, he'd have control over his body and the ways in which he wanted to experience the world.

She drifted down the hall, peering into the bedrooms one by one. The front bedroom looked out on the street, and she watched as a few neighborhood kids rode by on bicycles. A sudden flash of memory made her smile—Will, riding off into the darkness on his bicycle, the night before she moved to El Paso. A lifetime ago.

She offered up a silent thanks to the man who'd given her so much. The sale of Will's home and belongings had made it possible for them to buy this house and had paid for a lot of sign-language lessons.

She hoped Will would be proud of the way she'd handled things and how she'd spent his money.

"Hey." Carter stole into the room behind her and wrapped his arms around her waist. Ben came running in a second later, gripping the ball.

"Doing okay?" Carter rested his chin on the top of her head as Ben dropped the ball and started chasing it.

Sophia smiled, leaning back against his solid frame. "Oh, yeah, I'm more than okay." She arched into him a little, earning a chuckle.

"Ma'am, are you trying to seduce me?"

"Yep," she said, running her hands along his arms. "Is it working?"

His breath was hot in her ear. "You know it is. We'll definitely have some fun tonight."

She shivered at the promise in his voice. "Good," she said. Ben's bedtime couldn't come soon enough.

"Is this going to be your study?" Carter asked. "It's got a nice view."

"It does," Sophia said. "But I was thinking we could use it for something else."

"Oh? What did you have in mind?"

"A nursery, maybe?"

Carter froze behind her, and she smiled. He dropped his arms and turned her to face him. "Soph, are you saying—?"

She shook her head, unable to keep him in suspense any longer. "No. Not yet. But maybe next year?" She'd be done with her research by then, and she'd already been offered a contract position at the university to continue her studies for a PhD. It was a tempting offer, and it would increase her chances of eventually working for NASA.

But as she watched her son play and saw the growing excitement on Carter's face, she knew she didn't have to have her dream job to have her dream life. She could find rewarding work in Austin. As long as she had this boy and this man by her side, nothing else mattered.

He nodded enthusiastically, grinning from ear to ear. "Yes," he said. "Absolutely. In fact, we should probably start practicing now, to make sure we know how it's done." He leaned down and kissed her, holding her close.

Sophia kissed him back, then swatted him away with a laugh. "Dial it back, cowboy. You know the rule." No hanky-panky until Ben was asleep. At fifteen months, he still required constant supervision.

Carter groaned good-naturedly. "Not fair," he said. "You can't spring something like that on me and expect me to not react."

"We'll have time for that later," she promised him. "Like after the furniture has arrived."

"Floors can be comfortable with the right person," he said silkily.

"You're definitely the right person for me," she told him. "But I'm still not sleeping on the floor."

"Who said anything about sleep?" Carter lifted his eyebrows suggestively and she couldn't help but laugh.

"It's a good thing I love you," she said.

"I love you, too," he said, reaching for her. He pressed a kiss to the top of her head as Ben ran around their legs, chasing the ball. "Now, and always."

* * * * *

Don't miss the previous installments of
Lara Lacombe's Rangers of Big Bend series:

The Ranger's Reunion Threat
Ranger's Baby Rescue
Ranger's Justice

Available now from Harlequin Romantic Suspense.

SPECIAL EXCERPT FROM

(H) HARLEQUIN

ROMANTIC SUSPENSE

*Journalist Neema Kamau will risk anything to uncover
the truth. She'll even get close to politician Davis Black
in order to investigate his possible organized crime
connections. But when her professional interest turns
personal, the stalker who's circling them both might rob
her of the chance to make things right...*

Read on for a sneak preview of
Stalked by Secrets,
the next thrilling romance in
Deborah Fletcher Mello's
To Serve and Seduce miniseries.

Neema suddenly sat upright, pulling a closed fist to her
mouth. "I'm sorry. There's something we need to talk
about first..." she started. "There's something important
I need to tell you."

Davis straightened, dropping his palm to his crotch to
hide his very visible erection. "I'm sorry. I was moving
too fast. I didn't mean—"

"No, that's not—"

Titus suddenly barked near the front door, the fur
around his neck standing on end. He growled, a low,
deep, brusque snarl that vibrated loudly through the
room. Davis stood abruptly and moved to peer out the
front window. Titus barked again and Davis went to the
front door, stopping first to grab his gun.

Neema paused the sound system, the room going quiet save Titus's barking. She backed her way into the corner, her eyes wide. She stood perfectly still, listening to see if she could hear what Titus heard as she watched Davis move from one window to another, looking out to the street.

"Go sit," Davis said to the dog, finally breaking through the quiet. "It's just a raccoon." He heaved a sigh of relief as he turned back to Neema. "Sorry about that. I'm a little on edge. Since that drive-by, every strange noise makes me nervous."

"Better safe than sorry," she muttered.

Davis moved to her side and kissed her, wrapping his arms tightly around her torso. "If I made you uncomfortable before, I apologize. I would never—"

"You didn't," Neema said, interrupting him. "It was fine. It was…good…and I was enjoying myself. I just… well…" She was suddenly stammering, trying to find the words to explain herself. Because she needed to come clean about everything before they took things any further. Davis needed to know the truth.

Don't miss
Stalked by Secrets *by Deborah Fletcher Mello,*
available March 2021 wherever
Harlequin Romantic Suspense
books and ebooks are sold.

Harlequin.com